Alice Dippleblack in

On The Run

By
K. J. Bailey

Second Edition

This is a work of fiction. Names, characters, places, and incidents either are the products of the author's imagination or are used fictitiously. Any resemblance to actual persons, living or dead, businesses, companies, events, or locales is entirely coincidental.

ISBN: 978-0-9978858-3-5

Chapter 1

Rabaroo

"So, where're we goin' exactly?" Alice asks her friends, hoisting her full shoulder bag back into place again. With her brace of waterskins, core stone weighted backpack, and sword sling, there really wasn't much room left on the slim girl's shoulders. This meant that every time she adjusted under the weight of her gear, the sky blue shoulder bag eagerly slid down her sunset furred arm.

Being a Tokala, Alice Dippleblack has many features in common with her fox ancestors. Her fine fur very much resembles the coloring of the red fox, down to the black coating the tips of her triangular ears, forearms, and feet. She even has a thick full tail tipped in snowy white poking out of a slit in her trousers.

Danahlia half turns to the fox girl from a few steps ahead, though with the hood of her brown traveling cloak up, Alice can only see the end of the lizard girl's tapering muzzle as she smirks, "Northeast."

Alice snorts, "I know that, but are we headin' toward a village or somethin', or are we just wanderin'?"

"Mostly wanderin'," Danahlia calls back cheerily.

"Danny! Keep your tail under your cloak!" Twinkaleni chides at Alice's side. The diminutive mouse girl grabs at the Liguna's long brown appendage as it uncurls from under the garment to swish free in a low arch.

Danahlia lifts it out of the Murin's reach, "Relax, Twinkie. We haven't seen anyone all day. 'Sides, she needs to breathe."

In truth, the trio hadn't seen anyone since they left the pixie forest several days ago. Twinkaleni had made the plan to slip between the villages bordering the forest so as to leave no mention of their passing on anyone's lips. This way, whoever was pursuing them would have little to go by whenever they managed to navigate the vast forest that had been the trio's home for the last months.

Alice had grown up near the forest and was saddened to leave it behind. Before meeting Twinkaleni, former mage of the Order of

Thermathrogi, and Danahlia, a Cold Blood refugee, she had lived a simple, if somewhat lonely, life at the edge of one of the smaller villages bordering the vast forest. She had been trying to make a living by hunting local monsters known as jellies. Each of these hemispherical blobs possessed a pearl like core stone that the young Tokala could trade for whatever she might need. She had to hunt, as she no parents to look after her. They had both perished because of the current war.

Twinkaleni called it the Blood War because the fighting was between the cold blooded people of Feoria and the warm blooded people of Arsalia. This conflict left Alice alone to fend for herself at an early age. She struggled but managed to get by, often with the help of her friend, Ashleigh, and her kind mother. The Didels had been there for Alice through some difficult times and leaving her village was hard predominately because it meant not being able to see them anymore, even though the actual decision to do so was largely taken out of her hands.

After meeting Danahlia and Twinkaleni by chance on one of her jelly hunting expeditions, Danahlia had been captured by a few of Toki village's remaining citizens. The lizard girl, being a Cold Blood caught in a Warm Blood village, was in real danger before Alice and Twinkaleni managed to rescue her. Being seen aiding a Cold Blood had marked Alice as a traitor to anyone who knew her face, forcing her to flee with her new friends from the only home she had ever known. News of the incident might have traveled to other villages, which was another reason Twinkaleni had the girls skirting past the settlements around the forest when they made their break from it.

Alice would have very much preferred staying in the forest. The girls had made many friends among the local pixies and feral animals that dwelt there. They also had a dry place to sleep, fresh food, and clean water, but the news that someone hunting Twinkaleni had entered the forest inspired them to flight once more.

The youngest and by far the smallest of the trio, Twinkaleni, none the less, possessed incredible magical powers. She had been raised in, what seemed to Alice, an abominable prison/school for those gifted with magic. While being trained to fight in the Blood War, Twinkaleni had managed to escape and was now being pursued by some agent of the awful institution. Unwilling to risk an encounter with the unknown but likely formidable foe, the girls opted to run and now travel somewhat aimlessly across the country.

Twinkaleni leaps at Danahlia's upraised tail, squeaking angrily, "Danny, if someone sees you're a Liguna there will be severe consequences!"

"Come on, Twinkie, lighten up. We're in the middle o' nowhere," Danahlia jeers, bobbing her tail just out of the Murin's reach.

Under the weight of her pack, the tiny mouse girl can't jump very high. Her enormous round ears flop about with the effort, until she gives up to address Alice's previous question, "We just need to create as much distance as we can between us and whoever the Order has sent after me. Other than that, I don't really know where our destination should be."

"We still have some food, we should be ok for a little while," adds Danahlia, relaxing her tail to let it drag along the grass behind her.

The tallest and at sixteen, the oldest of the three, Danahlia Smoothide strides confidently onward, leading, as she generally likes to. From a distance, and if she bothered to conceal her lengthy tail, she would look as any traveler might under a large simple cloak. But up close, anyone would plainly see her unique features.

Danahlia is a Liguna. As such, the lizard girl shares many features with her reptilian kin. She is lean and long limbed with skin similarly patterned to an oak tree's bark, though very smooth to the touch. She has a rounded muzzle and eyes the color of fresh grass. Her fingers are tipped with gray, near black, claws the same color as her feet's large, curved talons. Like the other two in her party, Danahlia carries a backpack on her shoulders, though she also has a spear made with a sturdy stick and the sharp tip of a giant crab's leg. She uses it now as a walking aid but also to point out various animals and birds she spots.

Following Danahlia is Twinkaleni Orbear, a tiny Murin of twelve. The mouse girl's well kept fur is light gray with a near white countershading. She has bare, flesh pink hands and feet that occasionally peak out from under her oversized shirt and trousers. Being small, even for her kind, the girls had difficulty finding the mage clothes that fit. Because of this, Twinkaleni must spend time rolling up sleeves and leggings while also keeping various bits of rope tied to keep her too large garments from sliding off her tiny frame.

Alice grins down at the little mouse beside her. The girl's great round ears wave some with each step, reminding the Tokala of wings. Along with her pink nose, long white whiskers, large amber eyes, and oversized clothes, Twinkaleni looks adorable. The small mage peers up at her, cocking an eyebrow, "What?"

"Nothing," replies Alice, looking away at the surrounding trees to hide her smile, "So you guys haven't been this way before?"

The girls travel through a wooded area that didn't seem dense enough to be considered a true forest.

"I don't think so," Danahlia calls back from in front, looking around.

Alice had originally thought they were traveling a similar route to the one the other two had taken to get to her forest near Toki village. She asks, "Is this how you traveled before we met?"

"Sort of. We had maps before, so we had an idea of where we were goin' then," Danahlia replies.

"Oh right," says Alice, recalling the girls mentioning losing much of their belongings upon encountering the jellies that inhabited her forest.

As their trek continues, Alice takes a drink from one of her waterskins. It's late summer now and the warm air keeps the trio thirsty, even in the frequent shade of trees.

Danahlia lifts a skin over her head to drain what's left in it and then calls, "Shout out if you guys see water."

Only they don't find any at all.

The girls wander until the sun dips below the tree line. They then sit in a loose circle, sighing in relief, as their tired bare feet are finally given a chance to rest. They eat some of the fruit given to them by the pixies with rationing in mind despite their ever growing hunger. The sweet juices have Alice eager for more but she forces herself to have only a few pieces before closing off her backpack. With their dwindling supply of water and no idea when they'll be able to refresh it, the young Tokala can't even drink as much as she'd like. She sees the same sense of dissatisfaction in her companions as they settle in for the night and knowing she isn't alone gives her some small comfort.

In the evenings, Twinkaleni would often practice her enchanting, unintentionally turning a few more of their core stones into acrid smelling puddles of charred, quickly hardening goop. Tonight though, she seems far too tired, instead resting her head on her pack while laying spread eagle in the grass, much like the other two.

It's on all their minds but Alice gives it voice, "We need water."

"And food," Danahlia adds.

"Maps, too, would be helpful," Twinkaleni includes, "I think we should begin searching for a settlement, some small town or village."

This was something the girls had been avoiding thus far on their journey. The last time they had tried to trade for supplies in a village, Danahlia was nearly killed and Alice was branded a traitor.

"Think we're far enough away from Toki?" asks Alice.

"Considering word of our previous transgression would likely only be spread by the very few traveling merchants still braving the roads in these troubled times and the mere fact that we are far from any major trading hubs, it is quite likely that we will not be recognized if we ventured into a small enough community," explains Twinkaleni.

Danahlia lets out a breath, "Pretty sure that was a yes or no question."

Twinkaleni narrows her eyes at the larger girl, "Then yes, I think we should be safe as long as *you* remain hidden this time."

Danahlia snorts, rolls to her side, and flops the end of her lengthy tail over Twinkaleni's face. Immediately, she cries out in surprise and pain, yanking her tail from the little mage's open mouth.

"Ow! That *hurt*!" Danahlia exclaims, bringing her tail in close to examine the teeth marks Twinkaleni left in it.

"Serves you right," the Murin shoots back, wiping away a bit of spittle from her lips with a forearm as she puts her back to the lizard girl.

"Oh, you are gonna get it now, tiny," Danahlia declares, somehow leaping over to the much smaller girl. Before Twinkaleni can react, Danahlia grabs up the mouse mage in a full body hug, wrapping her arms, legs, and tail around the Murin. Twinkaleni squirms and wriggles, letting out little squeaks of distress but Danahlia holds her tight, rubbing a cheek over her captive's forehead, saying, "Nope, for that, you're mine for the night."

The mouse mage squirms for a bit more but eventually gives up, her tiny arms and legs poking out between Danahlia's. Alice finds herself grinning at the pair's unusual bond. Hungry, thirsty, but happy to be among friends, she goes to sleep.

Alice wakes the next morning feeling something soft and cold on her nose. Blurry vision reveals strange, yellow eyes looking into hers. She jumps, startling a small, furry feral. It's mostly light brown with tan tufts of fluff at the ends of two long, slender, upraised ears. Alice can make out few other details as it rises on hind legs, thicker than its tiny arms, and hops off with remarkable speed. She must have gasped at the sight of it because Twinkaleni, who has managed to extract herself from Danahlia's grasp at some point, looks to her with both large ears perked up in alarm.

"Are you alright?" the little mouse mumbles.

"Yeah, there was a thing," Alice blurts, pointing after the creature.

Twinkaleni's head cocks to one side, "A what?"

"Uh, a feral," her dry tongue sticks to her mouth, making it difficult to speak.

Danahlia stretches, "Hngh, did it look edible?"

Alice grins, "I guess, but it was fast, really fast."

"Fast food, huh? Maybe we can get one with our bows," suggests Danahlia.

Twinkaleni sputters, putting a hand to her mouth to try to cover a laugh that gets her looks from the other two girls.

"What?" Danahlia grumbles.

"Oh, nothing, nothing. I'm sure your efforts will be, most rewarding," the mouse mage grins widely.

Among other things, Alice and Danahlia brought the makeshift bows and arrows they had been working on since their more relaxing days in the pixie forest. They were of dubious quality, but could send an arrow a decent distance on occasion.

While having their meager breakfast, Alice describes the creature and the girls plan their first hunt since leaving the forest.

"If there was one, there are probably more. I imagine such creatures would prefer the safety of numbers," Twinkaleni suggests, taking a modest sip from a waterskin.

"And that means they'd have to be getting water from somewhere," adds Alice.

"True," Danahlia agrees, "and I bet they taste good after a few twirls over a fire, too."

Their supplies low and options limited, the trio leaves most of their belongings beside a particularly large tree and set off.

Now that they were looking for them, they find the small furry ferals everywhere. The tufts of fluff at the end of their long ears tend to give them away in the overgrown grasses, but those same ears seem to allow them to hear the girls' approach, even as they attempt to sneak up on them. Twinkaleni is right in that they are communal animals. The one that hears the girls' approaching lets off a shrill, undulating cry that alerts the others just before hopping away to then vanish among the brush.

"Ugh, this food is *too* fast," Danahlia complains as they lose sight of another.

Twinkaleni nods, "Indeed, but do you see how their ears shift about as they hop? I believe that is how they maintain the balance that allows them to leap so swiftly while staying upright. Those tufts at the ends may even be weighted or used to catch the air for added control. It's really very eff-"

Danahlia cuts her off, "Study 'em after we catch'em."

The small mage narrows her eyes at the Liguna, "Hmph, I wouldn't expect *you* to properly appreciate the acquisition of knowledge, but the more we learn, the more effectively we can hunt our quarry. Wouldn't you agree, Alice?"

Alice is about to when Danahlia beats her tail on the ground, "What's that supposed ta mean?"

Scanning around, Twinkaleni replies matter-of-factly, "I refer to your tendency to act without thinking, which has frequently led to your failure in various endeavors."

"Are you sayin' I'm stupid?!" Danahlia grumbles, approaching the much smaller girl.

Twinkaleni turns to look at her, standing her ground, "Oh, no. I'm saying you-"

"Guys, look!" Alice interrupts, as much to placate the situation as to announce a discovery.

"So, what? It's a hole," Danahlia says, glancing over, unimpressed.

"Ugh, she means to point out what I have suspected for some time. The creatures must be using burrows like these to hide in," Twinkaleni illuminates.

"Yeah, that's how come they keep disappearin'. They're not just fast, they're underground," Alice adds, kneeling to peer into the hole she can nearly stick her head into.

"You wanna dig 'em out?" Danahlia asks, crouching beside the Tokala.

The mouse mage announces, "I believe I may have an alternative. Excuse me."

The two taller girls give her some room and Twinkaleni approaches the hole. She raises both small arms over her head, fingers splayed, and then swings them down as if attempting to plug the hole with an invisible boulder, the act in unison with her shout of, "Vespis flowmino!"

A sudden powerful gust from behind and somehow above makes Alice jump and she needs to brace herself from being sucked into the hole. From the corner of her eye she sees movement in many directions. Looking up, the fox girl spots multiple geysers of dirt and dust fling several of the long eared, hopping beasts a few feet into the air. They cry out in surprise before plopping on the ground, dazed for only a second, before they dash back into their burrows.

Danahlia laughs out loud, "Ha! Not bad, Twinkie."

"Wags!" Alice cheers. "How'd you get 'em to pop up like that?"

Twinkaleni needs to take a few breaths before huffing out, "As I thought. The burrows, are all, connected."

"We got you now, hoppin' meat. Alice, you and me can wait by their holes, then Twinkie can launch 'em up again. If we're lucky, we can grab 'em before they dive."

"Right," Alice agrees, heading out to find another hole. Twinkaleni nods, still taking in mouthfuls of air.

Alice finds another of the holes and alerts Danahlia. The Liguna also finds one and then calls to Twinkaleni, "All set, Twinkie! Toss 'em!"

Alice looks over to the small mouse as she makes the same motions as before, though much slower, and wonders how much the Murin mage has left in her. Alice knew little about magic but from what she had seen and heard from Twinkaleni, casting spells can take a tremendous amount of effort and these wind spells were impressive workings. She is thinking this when a powerful burst of air and sand takes her on the cheek, knocking her onto her butt.

Pain lances up her spine the moment she hits the ground, her tail being squished under her. She coughs and spits gritty granules of sand while wiping the same from her face and rolling to the side to free the fluffy appendage. Blinking rapidly to clear her vision, she spots a large blur float up into the air and knows it must be one of the ferals shot free from its lair. Immediately, Alice covers the hole with her feet and reaches for the blur while squinting through the stinging dust. Her fingers grasp something solid and she tightens her grip, pulling it away from a shower of sand.

Alice takes a few steps, still spitting sand and brushing it from her furred face. The thing in her hand squirms frantically and she brings it up to examine her catch. She has one of the long eared creatures by a boney rabbit like foot. It dangles upside down, twisting to free itself from her grip. She looks at it struggling to reach her fingers, though it can't quite manage.

She then hears Danahlia cheer, "Hey guys, I got one! They're kinda cu- OW! It bit me!"

Alice turns to see the Liguna on the ground, reaching up to her shoulder into the hole she had been guarding, demanding, "Get back here you evil little meat creature!"

Alice laughs as Danahlia gives up, shouting into the hole, "I know where you live!"

Alice returns her attention to the struggling animal in her hand, its efforts to free itself slowing as it tires and gives in to its fate. She is suddenly racked with guilt and visions of the rat man they had slain back in the pixie forest. The young fox hadn't told the others but ever since then she had been struggling with the memories of what they had done. The Rotan was an awful person, but a person none the less, a person who was now dead because of her.

She is only allowed to dwell on such thoughts for a moment as Danahlia jogs up beside her, calling, "Oh wags, you got one!"

Alice is pulled back to the moment, turns to the larger girl, and nearly drops the weakly shifting beast. Danahlia takes it and immediately breaks its neck with a sudden twist of her hands, ending the unfortunate feral.

She then holds it up high to where Twinkaleni was standing to show off the reward of their efforts, shouting, "We're eatin' tonight!" but the little mage is gone. "Twinkie?" Danahlia calls out as Alice pulls her eyes from the now still beast to scan for the Murin.

They race back to where she was to find their gray furred companion collapsed in the grass. Both call to the little mouse girl, dropping to their knees beside her. The Murin's breathing is heavy but her eyes are closed.

"I think she's ok, just over did it with those spells," offers Danahlia, cradling the little mouse's head in her lap.

"What should we do?" Alice asks, taking up a small pink hand.

"She just needs a break," Danahlia assures, "Let's go get our stuff and cook this little monster up."

Alice helps Danahlia put Twinkaleni on the larger girl's back to be carried. The Liguna hunches over, supporting the downed mage with her tail as they head back to where they left their supplies, Alice carrying their bows and arrows along with their catch. As they walk, the gentle breeze that had been blowing sporadically for much of the day becomes steadily stronger. Looking up, Alice watches a few dark clouds float lazily across the afternoon sky. Her attention falls again on the limp furry feral in her hand and she wonders why Danahlia seemed to find it so easy to kill things.

For the most part, the lizard girl had been the one to finish off anything they had hunted. Alice had made kills too, but only things that were a threat. Jellies didn't count in her mind but she had slain her share of giant spiders and ants. Perhaps these where easier because they were so alien, so different from her. Ants and spiders didn't really cry out or show fear, but the long eared animal certainly did. Something the young fox now found haunting her thoughts along with the rat man.

"How do you do it?" Alice asks abruptly, watching the gathering clouds.

Danahlia looks over to her, "Huh?"

"How do you kill things so easily? You just broke this little guy's neck like it was nothin'," Alice replies, giving the dead beast a slight shake.

Danahlia purses her lips in thought for a second, "I don't like it if that's what you're thinkin'."

Alice looks over at her in surprise, "But you just snapped its ne-"

"Yeah, you should kill your prey quickly. No needless pain, no prolonged fear of death. Causing prey to suffer is disrespectful. The gift of life needs to be honored."

"What?"

"My dad taught me that. I never like killing things, but we need to if we plan to survive. You'll figure it out. It's either us or them, and I kinda like us."

"But it's like you don't even care about 'em," Alice nearly whispers, thinking the furred weight in her hands was breathing only a while ago, living it's life, trying to survive, and might have even had children to look after.

Danahlia snorts, "It's not that I don't care, but you have to think of your own. It sucks that things have to die, but everything does, so what does it matter when?"

Alice looks to the Liguna, "Your own?"

"Mm-hm. Because we caught that fuzz ball, Twinkie 'll eat," she gives the slumbering mouse on her back a smile, "And so will we. We're on our own out here, no more pixie food delivery service. Either we get food or we go hungry, and I'm not a fan o' hungry."

Alice lets out a little laugh, "Yeah, I know."

Danahlia grins at the fox girl then looks ahead, only to suddenly crouch. Alice follows suit, looking to where the girls had left their things. Around a great oak's trunk are their packs, and rummaging around them are several of the long eared animals. The Liguna gives the bows over Alice's shoulder a meaningful look and then jerks her head toward the beasts. Alice nods, carefully setting down her catch and hunting gear. She then takes her bow and nocks an arrow as swiftly and quietly as she can. Staying low, she draws the bow string, made of woven plant fibers, and takes aim.

Alice notices several of the animals have bits of what's left of the trio's dwindling store of fruit. She sights one munching on a blue adonseea and draws her bow all the way back to her cheek. The wood of the bow creaks under the stress and a few of the beasts great ears perk up as their owners look her way. Several shrill warning cries have the fruit raiders immediately hopping in every direction. With the element of surprise gone, Alice lets loose her arrow at the nearest of the beasts only to have it fly well over its head and out of sight. Before she can nock another arrow, the creatures are gone.

"Ticks!" Alice exclaims, lowering her bow.

"Agh! Those little monsters were eatin' our food!" Danahlia grumbles, rising to hurry over to their supplies. Together, they lower Twinkaleni into some grass to rest. Alice then runs off to look for her arrow before she forgets where it went.

She spots the bright yellow feather fletching, donated by some of the birds back in the pixie forest, sticking up from a tall bit of grass and races over to it. She jolts in surprise when she finds the arrow is sticking out of one of the long eared fruit thieves. The arrow caught the creature under a forelimb and has sunk deep into its chest. Even so, the animal is still alive, its body curled around the projectile, shivering.

"Oh no, I'm so sorry," Alice whimpers, falling to her knees by the creature's side.

The small animal shivers even more, its eyes locked on Alice but it clearly can't move beyond that. Her breathing quickens as her thoughts tell her to call out for Danahlia or perhaps to even try nursing the poor creature back to health, but in her heart she knows the wound is too great. She then remembers what the Liguna had said about not causing needless pain or fear. Her heart racing, the young fox grabs the dying animal. It struggles weakly but only for a second, its neck breaking with a swift jerk of Alice's hands. The still weight drops from shaking fingers.

Through blurred vision, Alice looks at what she has done and tears begin to run down her cheeks. "I'm sorry, I'm sorry, I'm sorry..." she repeats over and over, trembling at the sight of her hands, stained with a small bit of blood.

A few minutes later, she hears Danahlia calling for her. Wiping away tears on her dirty blouse sleeve, she sniffs, trying to regain her composure. Forcing her breathing to slow, Alice pulls free her arrow, picks up the dead animal, and heads back to her friends.

"AL-! Oh hey, did you find your ar-? Whoa, you got one?!" Danahlia asks as the Tokala shambles toward her.

Alice forces a grin, "Yeah, looks like we got two for dinner."

"*You* got two! You might almost be as skilled a hunter as me!" Danahlia congratulates with her usual sense of modesty.

Alice gives a little laugh, handing the lizard girl her kill, "How's Twinkaleni?"

"Still out. Let's get these guys skinned and gutted so we can eat."

The girls settle down with an animal each, trying to figure out the best way to clean them. This is a fairly new chore to Alice, who has only seen others doing it a few times. Danahlia, however, works with experienced hands, pulling the furred skin of the animal's legs apart first and then working down to strip much of the rest off in one long pull. Alice imitates her and, with some effort, manages a similar result.

With the forearm length soldier ant mandibles the girls acquired in the pixie's forest, they clean out the ferals and then work to prepare a fire. While doing this, they discuss what to call the beasts.

"Nah, dust bunnies is too cutesy. Remember, we gotta eat these guys. How 'bout dirt devils?" Danahlia suggests.

"They're not evil," Alice counters with a smirk.

"Uh, they are so. One totally bit me."

"You were gonna to kill it and eat it."

"So. It didn't know that."

"I think it could guess."

"Fine, what about dirt hoppers?" Danahali offers, sticking a stick through one to use as a spit.

"Mm, better," says Alice, trying to get a few decent sparks with her flint and steel. She recalls a pictured book she had seen with various ferals in it. One image stands out because its feet were long just like their dinner's. It started with a K but she can't- "Kangaroo! Kangaroo rabbit," she blurts when the name finally hits her.

Danahlia raises a brow, "Kangaroo rabbit? Kinda long, how about kabbit, or kangabit? Oh! Rabaroo!"

"Ha! Rabaroo, I like it," Alice smiles. She then notices a tiny wisp of smoke coiling up from the crushed dried leaves she is trying to light and immediately begins to blow on it, gently and steadily, until a small flame emerges. Nursing the flame to strength with more dead leaves, she manages to start their cooking fire.

"Wags!" Danahlia cheers, "We have a name and a fire. Rabaroo!"

Chapter 2

Chickenwoods

As their rabaroos cook over the fire, Alice looks to Twikaleni who still slumbers in the grass. It's late in the afternoon, but with the gathering clouds, it feels much later.

"Think she's ok? Magic wears her out I know, but she's been sleepin' for a long time now."

"She's fine. Just went a little overboard today is all," Danahlia says, reaching back to pet the little mouse's head gingerly.

"Has she ever collapsed like that before?" Alice asks, unable to shake the worry in her gut for their youngest companion.

"Once I've seen. This was way back before we met. Me and Twinkie were hikin' through a pretty dense bit of woods when we start hearin' these sounds comin' from the trees, like darkly chitterin' squirrels. We're ignorin' it for the most part, figurin' it's just some ferals, but every little while, it comes back, and louder."

"What was it?" Alice asks, turning her rabaroo over the fire.

"Twinkie called 'em chechies when we spotted one. Small, nasty, hairy things that hid around trees and bushes, so we couldn't see 'em clearly. Thing is, every time we heard 'em chitterin' in that dark way of theirs, their numbers grew. More and more gathered just on the edge o' sight, stayin' hidden, but we knew they were there. See, the more that gathered, the more shapes we'd see dartin' between trees, the more twigs we'd hear snapping under their hairy little feet, and the louder they'd chitter."

"What happened?" Alice wonders, now thoroughly enthralled by the tale.

Danahlia smirks toward the little mage, "Twinkie said these chechies were known to be cowardly, so they were gatherin' up their numbers to attack. She seemed pretty sure we'd be safe if we made it outta their territory so we picked up the pace, takin' it to a jog, and then a full run. But those nasty little things kept right on with us, musterin' their strength the whole way. The chitterin' got so loud at one point I could swear there had to be a hundred of 'em out trackin' us."

Danahlia grins, seeing Alice's pointed fox ears angled toward her with undivided interest, and continues, "Runnin' for our lives now, an army of these chechi critters chasin' after us, the chitterin' suddenly stops. Nothin' moves, no twigs break, no leaves rustle, no nothin'. The silence is so strange and heavy that we stop too, wonderin' what was goin' on. Then out of a bush leaps the biggest, ugliest, and hairiest of the bunch, charging in and screamin' some kinda battle cry. All the others join in too, right on his heels, all screamin' at the tops of their lungs."

Alice's eyes widen and Danahlia goes on.

"Just as the leader's nearly on us, Twinkie throws up a hand and hits him with a ball of fire so hot it turns him to ash mid leap, straight dusts 'im right there," she says, her fingers making a bursting motion, "As a few charred bones clatter to the ground, the other hundred or so panic and run off into the trees."

"Wow," Alice exclaims, looking back to her roasting dinner.

"She passed out after that, only other time. But she woke up a little after, hungry as I've ever seen her. Said it had to do with some guy's fat or somethin'."

"Mana fatigue," Twinkaleni mumbles.

"Yeah, that was... Twinkie!" Danahlia cries, turning to the weakly shifting Murin.

Alice crawls over to their smallest companion and both girls stroke her fur gently, "Are you ok?"

Twinkaleni opens her mouth several times, her tongue working as if trying to moisten it and then croaks, "Ugh, is there any water left?"

"Yeah, yeah, here," Danahlia says, lifting the little girl's head into her lap before bringing a waterskin to her lips. The mouse mage drains what's left in the skin and the other two share a relieved smile.

"How do you feel?" Alice asks, stroking one tiny bare hand between her own.

"Oh, tired. Something smells good," the Murin groans, her nose sniffing the air.

"Ha, yeah. Alice caught us some dinner. You hungry?" asks Danahlia, recapping the waterskin.

"Quite," Twinkaleni replies.

Once the mouse mage can sit up on her own, the girls have a meal of browning fruit and meat. It's the most they've had in a little while and they all eat with gusto, Danahlia insisting they eat the fruit already gotten into by the rabaroo. The meat turns out a little stringy but is also tender, warm, and filling. The girls have trouble stopping their feast, but do so at Alice's suggestion and put half of one animal away for later along with a few last handfuls of fruit.

It's dark when the girls settle down around their fire for the night. The trees in the area have been too spindly to risk trying to sleep in so they lie in patches of soft grass, heads on their backpacks, looking up at the blanket of clouds looming over them.

"Probably gonna rain soon," yawns Alice.

"It would be a boon considering we're nearly out of water," says Twinkaleni.

Danahlia yawns too, "As long as it holds off till mornin'."

"We should seek shelter. Who knows how long it might last," Twinkaleni advises.

"Good idea," Alice agrees.

"In the mornin'," Danahlia says sleepily and the girls soon drift off.

Alice finds the wounded Rabaroo shivering on the ground, her flimsy wooden arrow sticking up from its chest. She picks it up and jerks its head and body in opposite directions as she had before to end its suffering. But it doesn't work. Her efforts only cause it more pain. She tries again and again but the poor little beast only screeches in agony as blood begins to run over her hands and forearms.

"It's not working!" she cries in apology, the little animal letting out horrible pained shrieks as she tries again and again, it's legs kicking wildly, "I can't! I'm sorry! I-I can't do it! I'm sorry! I'm so sorry!"

She's jolted from the nightmare by a rumble of thunder.

Alice breathes deeply and rapidly, grateful for the escape, and looks around in the dark of a cloudy early morning to find her companions awakened as well. They lay in silence for a moment, uninterested in getting up at this hour after so eventful a day, but another even louder rumble tells them that things are only getting started. Even so, Alice lies back down and closes her eyes, only to have another rumble pop them back open.

After a few moments, she hears Twinkaleni say what they all know, "We should begin seeking shelter from the coming storm."

"Might as well," Danahlia grumbles.

The girls eat breakfast while they walk, munching on what's left of their fruit.

Tired and frequently yawning, Alice asks Twinkaleni, who walks beside her, "How're you feelin'?"

"Meh, not bad," Danahlia answers before looking back from her lead position, "Oh."

The girls give her a look before Twinkaleni replies, "Better, thank you."

"You had us worried. Does using magic really take so much out of you?" Alice wonders of the little mage.

Twinkaleni nods, "It can, yes. It didn't help that I was already tired, and we really haven't been eating as well as back in the pixie's forest."

The Tokala tilts her head to one side, "I thought you used nature forces for your magic. Why does it wear you out so much?"

"Mmm, well, while a great deal of the energy in my spells does tend to come from my surroundings, the true skill of magic wielders is in how well we channel those energies into a desired effect."

Alice recalls Twinkaleni's first spell from yesterday, "Like when you shot air into the rabaroo hole. I felt the air around us being pushed into it. The wind didn't really come from you, instead you gathered the air that was around us and shoved it in."

"Yes, yes," Twinkaleni smiles, nodding approvingly, "Now you're starting to understand magical theory. Magic is not an act of creation but an act of manipulation, of alteration. Like a sculptor with clay. The clay is a formless mass on its own but with skilled hands an individual can turn it into a pot, a cup, a bowl, or any number of useful things."

Alice grins widely, glad to understand just a little more of Twinkaleni's amazing power. She raises her arms and spreads her fingers to feel the breeze that had been steadily building since the dark clouds above began to gather and then wonders, "But you can make fire when there isn't any around. How do you do that?"

"And what is fire but heat?" Twinkaleni answers, "And heat is all around us, in the summer air, on a sun baked stone, and even on the petals of flowers bathed in day light."

Alice's ears perk up, "You can get fire from flowers?"

"Certainly, though it would take quite a few of them to create an adequate enough flame to match even a candle. Perhaps you noticed the slightest temperature drop when I use my fire spell?" Alice hadn't and shakes her head, so Twinkaleni continues, "Mm, I wouldn't think so. You see, to create a flame hot enough to start a fire requires a tremendous amount of heat, not easily found in nature in any one place. Thus, to amass enough energy to create a flame of significance, I borrow the heat from a wide area and focus it in the smallest place possible. You may recall seeing it as a sort of beam."

"Yeah, yeah," Alice nods, recalling the many times TwInkaleni had used her fire spell to light their camp fires. "Is that what makes it so tiring? Taking in energy from all over? Manafats?"

The mouse mage gives Danahlia a displeased look, correcting Alice, "Mana fatigue. Honestly, Danny, 'some guy's fat'?"

"What? You say a lot o' things, I can't be responsible for rememberin' all of it," the Liguna tosses back.

"And I recall facing no more than three chechies that day, none particularly formidable," Twinkaleni says, still eyeing the larger girl.

"Oh there were more. You just couldn't see 'em runnin' around in the bushes 'cause you're too short." Twinkaleni narrows her eyes at Danahlia who goes on to say, "Anyway, it sounds better the way I tell it."

"Indeed," the mouse mage says shortly.

Alice grins at the exchange and then asks, "What's mana?"

"Oh, yes. Mana is the raw natural energy a mage possesses and is somewhat similar to one's stamina but is exhausted only when using magic. Those touched with magic use their own store of mana to channel and manipulate the energies he or she gathers. The greater or more complex a working, the more mana is consumed," Twinkaleni explains.

Alice picks up on the stamina part and wonders, "It's like getting tired after you run?"

"In a sense yes, that's precisely what it's like. A brisk walk over a short distance uses only a little stamina. But running as fast as you can for as long as you can is a greater effort. Expending mana tires the body similarly to such physical exertions."

"Oh. Do you get it back? Your mana?" the inquisitive fox asks further.

"You do. Very similarly to your stamina, some rest will help restore it, keeping well fed and hydrated help speed things along as well," Twinkaleni smiles. "And you may find this fascinating. The more-" Danahlia makes a disinterested sound with her tongue, but Twinkaleni lets it pass, "The more you use mana, the more you can exert, after proper recovery of course."

"Like muscles. The more you use 'em, the stronger they get and the more you can do," Alice adds, flexing her own arm.

"Yes, exactly!" Twinkaleni bubbles, seeming very pleased to have someone interested in magic to talk to.

The girls wander on for much of the day, Alice and Twinkaleni talking while Danahlia leads them on into the unknown. Learning from Twinkaleni helps Alice forget about the girl's rather uncertain circumstances, until a ground shaking crash of thunder has them all ducking.

"Ticks, that sounded close," exclaims Danahlia.

"At least it's not rainin' yet," says Alice, looking around cautiously and noting she hadn't seen any animals about today.

"A boon and a curse," grumbles Twinkaleni, picking up her waterskin from where she dropped it, dismally watching what little was left inside being swallowed by the parched earth.

"Here," Alice says, offering the last of her own water, her tongue sticking to the roof of her mouth. She tries and fails to moisten it, her throat too dry to come up with any saliva. Twinkaleni accepts the water gratefully, taking just a sip but still emptying the skin. She hands it back apologetically, but Alice only smiles as the girls continue on.

Thunder frequently rumbles overhead. This is occasionally accompanied by lightning ripping across the darkened sky, causing Alice to duck, her ears pointing to the ground and tail tucking between her legs. Perhaps because of her great ears or that she is still very young, Twinkaleni seems especially affected by the cracks of thunder and walks with her ears folded against the sides of her head, jumping with each crash. Danahlia, however, stomps on in her ever confident manner, determined to get her companions to safety. By late afternoon though, even Danahlia's pace has slowed, her shoulders sag, and she leans more heavily on her spear.

The Liguna looks back to see her friends have fallen behind and waits for them to catch up before rasping, "Anyone got any more water?"

Before either girl can respond in the negative, a flash of lightning paints the world white and is followed almost instantly by another frightfully powerful crash of thunder. Twinkaleni falls to her knees with a squeak of distress, holding her large ears folded against her head as hard as she can, shivering in fright. Alice crouches beside the Murin, wrapping her in both arms before shaking her head at their reptilian companion.

Danahlia looks up at the menacing clouds angrily and screams, "YOU'VE BEEN RUMBLIN' ALL FLEA BITTEN DAY! EITHER RAIN OR MOVE ON ALREADY!"

She then glares at the sky, daring a response. Startled by the Liguna's outburst, Alice looks up too, only to flinch when a wet drop hits her over one eye. The first few drops are so unexpected that Alice wipes at them, thinking some bugs where landing on her fur. But as more begin to fall, she looks around to see that it was finally raining. A drop hits her on the nose and she crosses her eyes to see it. Danahlia lifts a hand up in disbelief, feeling the light rainfall.

She and Alice share a look with widening grins and Twinkaleni steadily looks upward, "It's raining?"

"It's raining," Alice confirms.

"It's raining! Maybe I *can* use magic eh, Twinkie?!" Danahlia shouts, opening her mouth wide to catch a few drops.

The others join her, letting the falling water moisten their dried tongues. As they do, the rain strengthens, quickly becoming a downpour. The girls laugh and cheer, no longer minding the thunder, as they spread their arms to let the rain soak their clothes, fur, and skin.

Twinkaleni has Alice take out her little tent and the girls set it up upside so that the fabric catches the lifesaving water in a recess. Danahlia adds the crab shell bowl and the girls dance and laugh in the rain, waiting for them to fill. The moment there is any puddling in their receptacles, they eagerly sip it down, the cool liquid like a balm on prickly throats. After a little while, they can dunk in their empty waterskins, filling them to capacity for the first time since leaving the pixie forest. Their hydration needs finally met, the girls start to bathe.

The last few days were through dry dusty lands. Hiking all that way meant they all had their share of dirt and grime clinging to them. Danahlia strips down first, tossing off her rain soaked cloak then quickly removing her blouse and modified trousers, the original needing a much larger tail slit.

The Liguna stands, arms and legs spread without a hint of shame, feeling the water fall all over her before she begins rubbing herself down. Alice watches the lizard girl for a moment, her lips pursed by a tendril of jealousy for Danahlia's rather generous chest and other well developed feminine curves. It wasn't the first time Alice had seen them, but she was always a little envious, her own figure one of modest and slim proportions. Danahlia catches her watching and grins as the fox girl turns away under the guise of rubbing some grime from her forearm while silently reasoning that Danahlia *is* a few years older than she, so there was still time to grow.

Knowing there was next to no chance of anyone being out here in the middle of nowhere and in this weather, Alice begins stripping down to her fur too. Twinkaleni needs a bit of help getting undressed when her soaked shirt catches around her expansive ears, but soon the girls are free to clean themselves in the heavy rain. It feels wonderfully luxurious to scrub away the dirt and stink of the last days. Danahlia is done quickly, with no fur or hair at all to comb through, and begins placing all their dirty clothes into the pool made by Alice's inverted tent to soak and be washed.

What seemed a wonderful reprieve only a short time ago swiftly becomes a tremendous burden. Now cleaned and well hydrated, the abundance of water now serves to keep them wet and, with the sun setting somewhere behind the clouds, cold. The day waning, the dark clouds and unrelenting rain limits their visibility as they slog along. The relatively new clothes the girls change into are instantly soaked, becoming heavy and uncomfortable. The rain also turns the once dry earth into thick mud, further hampering the girl's efforts as they desperately seek shelter.

Keeping close together, Alice and Danahlia hold the fabric of Alice's tent over their heads, Twinkaleni between them. The waterproof cloth helps keep them from the worst of it, as they wander blindly along. Despite their efforts, the larger girls' legs keep knocking into Twinkaleni as they walk, the little mouse enduring it while trying to keep close enough to stay somewhat sheltered.

Alice is busy watching her footing, trying to match pace with the Murin to keep from stepping on her feet, when Danahlia calls, "Look!"

What might be a path cuts through some of the vegetation and winds through a few trees ahead. It's only barely distinct from the rest of the muddy ground and could very well just be a path made by passing ferals, but it's the only lead they have.

"Think we should follow it?!" Alice shouts, needing to over the roar of rain.

Twinkaleni says nothing, keeping her head down with her arms crossed over her tiny chest while trying to keep her ears folded against the sides of her head with both shoulders.

"Wherever it goes can't be any worse than anywhere else out here!" Danahlia shouts back.

With few other options, the girls get on the small path and hope for the best.

The path, somewhat barer than the ground they had been walking on, is a thick, muddy goop under foot. Eager to see where it leads, Danahlia quickens her pace, her taloned feet having no problem giving her traction. Alice and Twinkaleni try to keep up but with the continuing downpour, the mud quickly becomes a slick hazard. Twinkaleni slips, her short legs unable to keep up with the Liguna's demands and Alice tumbles over her. The Murin mage manages to catch herself with her hands but Alice, trying to keep her weight from falling onto the smaller girl, lands on her side hard. She yips in pain, her right elbow hitting a rock just below the murky water's surface.

"Alice!" Twinkaleni squeaks, crawling over to her.

In the tumble, Alice tore away the tent fabric from Danahlia who is forced to stop and now stands in the rain getting soaked, "Guys, stop playin' in the mud! I see somethin' ahead!"

"I think she's hurt, help her!" Twinakleni shouts.

"I'm fine, I'm fine!" Alice shouts back, rising to her feet, but the moment she extends her right arm, jagged pain shoots up her elbow. She gasps and has to keep the arm tucked in. Danahlia raises her left arm over her shoulder and holds her close in an effort to help her walk. "I'm fine! Really! I just hit my elbow!" Alice protests but Danahlia sticks by her anyway.

After a few assisted steps, Alice can make out a silhouette in the distance, too short and squat to be a tree. Upon seeing it, she calls, "I see somethin' over there!"

"I think it's a house!" says Danahlia.

Alice volunteers to scout it out.

"You sure?!" Danahlia asks.

Alice nods, "Yeah, you guys stay back here!"

"Danny! Cover yourself, who knows who might live in such a place!" warns Twinkaleni, having wrapped herself in the tent's fabric.

These being Warm Blood lands and Danahlia being of cold blood in a time when her people are considered enemies, the Liguna must be extra careful to keep herself from unfriendly eyes. She dawns her soaking wet cloak, putting up the hood, and wrapping her lengthy tail about her waist and legs while Alice presses on alone toward the small building.

It turns out to be a shack, simply made from wood and in a sad state of disrepair. From the look of it, Alice doesn't think anyone still lived here but that didn't mean nothing did. She draws her enchanted sword, Jellybane, awkwardly from the sheath on her back with her left hand as she approaches a window, a single shutter hanging below it on one valiant hinge. Alice ends up stepping on the other, it having fallen off at some point, as she peers in.

The inside of the shack is dark and looks long abandoned. Alice stabs the mud at her feet with the tip of her enchanted sword before reaching it into the shack. After a moment, the blade begins to glow green. The glow illuminates a few old wooden furnishings and little else.

"Hello!?" she calls loudly. She hears nothing over the rain and Jellybane, having cleansed itself of the mud, returns to its mundane state. Fairly sure it's safe the young Tokala waves her companions over.

The wooden door is warped with age and Danahlia ends up kicking it in frustration, causing the entire thing to fall into the building with a loud bang. The girls rush in, glad to finally have something solid over their heads. Alice dips her sword in mud once more, lighting the cramped, mold smelling dwelling.

It's only one room. A single wooden chair and table take up one corner and what might have been a bed long ago, now a garden of mushrooms and other fungi, takes up another. Alice can make out a dark recess made of stone in the furthest corner.

"A fire place!" she cries gleefully, her wet fur cold and heavy.

Danahlia lifts the wooden door back into its splintering frame and says over her shoulder, "Wags! Let's get it lit!"

There isn't any fire wood around and everything outside is soaking wet, so Danahlia takes the one wooden chair, lifting it back, before calling, "Heads up!"

Seeing what she plans, Twinkaleni and Alice both look away as the Liguna smashes the chair against the stone of the chimney. Pieces fly everywhere and for several minutes Twinkaleni and Danahlia crawl about tossing them into the fireplace. With one good arm, Alice can only hold the glowing sword for them. As they work, the fox girl does manage to find what may have been a table cloth or curtain. She grabs it with her toes and places it near the fireplace. Twinkaleni pushes the broken bits of wood off to the side to better avoid the rain falling into the chimney.

Danahlia places the old but dry bit of cloth near the base of the pile and then asks, "Got any fire left in ya, Twinkie?"

"I believe so. Stand back," the Murin commands. The girls do and with a shout of "Feasta!" the room chills briefly as a fire blossoms.

The thoroughly wet trio remove their dripping garments and backpacks around the fire. Twinkaleni and Alice shake vigorously, shedding the abundant moisture from their fur, their coats fluffing out in the effort. Danahlia adjusts the splintered wood to encourage the fire's growth but a sneeze nearly douses it. She sniffs and begins running her hands over her smooth skin to remove excess water.

The girls pile their belongings in a relatively dry spot, giving them some room to move around. The inside of the shack is fairly dry, with only a few spots leaking from the roof. One leak is in the corner near the door and Alice tries wringing the girl's clothes over the puddle under it, but sharp pains in her right elbow keep her from putting much effort into the task. Twinkaleni takes over for her as Danahlia removes what's left of their remaining Rabaroo from her pack, puts it in the crab shell bowl, and sits it by the fire.

Alice pokes at the mud below the open window to keep Jellybane lit while testing her hurting arm. She then wanders over to the mushrooms growing mostly from the wooden frame of the terribly rotted bed. Her sword casts the strangely shaped fungi in its green light, making many look black.

Danahlia joins her, sneezing again before asking, "(sniff) Think any o' these are edible?"

Alice had limited experience with mushrooms, though she knew some were poisonous. Before she could support herself hunting jellies, Alice had often foraged for things to eat in the fields around her small village as well as at the nearby forest's edge. If the young fox found anything that looked like food, she would race back to Toki with it and ask more experienced foragers if it was safe. If so, she would often give the plants or mushrooms to whoever was offering her bedding for the night to cook into the evening meal. As such, she knew that good mushrooms were wonderful in soups, but as for which ones *were* good, she knew she still had much to learn.

She spots one that looks familiar. "What about that one?" she asks, pointing to a particularly large formation of fungi growing in shelves on the side of the rotten, wooden frame. They look brown in the green light.

"Oh wags! Those are chickenwoods!" Danahlia cheers.

"Chickenwoods?" Twinkaleni asks, joining them.

"Yeah, because they taste kinda like chicken," says Alice excitedly, recalling the name.

The older girls immediately begin harvesting the fungi though Twinkaleni hesitates, "Are you quite sure these are of an edible variety?"

"Pretty sure," says Danahlia.

Alice adding, "Almost positive."

Twinkaleni sighs.

"How'd you wanna cook 'em?" Danahlia asks, grabbing a handful.

"We have a bowl, how about a soup?" Alice suggests.

In agreement, the girls rip the chickenwood caps and stalks into pieces, placing them in the crab shell bowl along with the Rabaroo. Danahlia then hangs the bowl out the window to collect water.

Once it's nearly full, they place the bowl atop the fire to cook.

All terribly hungry and with little else to be done, the girls gather around the small fire and wait for their meal. Danahlia sits in the middle, Twinkaleni and Alice on either side. The Liguna sneezes once more and it's then that Alice sees how much she's shaking. Without even dry clothes to offer, Alice scoots beside the shivering girl and leans into her to share her body heat. Twinkaleni does the same. Their fur is still damp but this close to the fire and huddled together, it doesn't take terribly long to dry. Danahlia puts her arms around both girls and holds them close. Alice can feel the lizard girl's tail tuck around her leg and she drapes her own fluffy tail over it. They all share a smile and Danahlia gives the furry girls a squeeze, she then sighs contentedly before sneezing again.

The rain continues unabated but the interior of the shack warms nicely. The fire crackles and sizzles as drops of rain hit it from the open chimney and slowly the aroma of their cooking meal begins to permeate the air. The girls' stomachs rumble as if talking to each other and when they can wait no more, they remove the bowl from the fire with their still damp clothes. All three blow eagerly on the steaming bowl, the scent only enticing them to further action.

Then Danahlia asks, "Anyone bring a spoon?"

They hadn't, so when the bowl is cool enough the girls take turns sipping from the contents. The water has taken on the flavor of the rabaroo and chickenwoods giving it a decent meaty taste, but what's more is that it's warm and filling. The mushrooms have become delicate with a slight chew to them and give their mouths something to do in between sips. Once the soup is gone, the three pick apart the rabaroo to the bones. Sated and exhausted, the girls lie back on the old wooden floor, huddled together, and fall asleep.

Chapter 3

Storm

Alice wakes first, or so she thinks. Looking around, the memory of were she is returning to her, she finds Twinkaleni once again wrapped in Danahlia's arms, legs, and a bit of her long tail, giving her a pleading look. It's an adorable sight, the lizard girl holding the little Murin like a beloved stuffed animal. Twinkaleni squirms, which only tightens the Liguna's grip as she mumbles softly in her sleep. A tiny furless hand extends toward Alice and she grasps it, grinning, to gently pull free the trapped Murin. Danahlia reluctantly lets her go, rolling to her belly with a disappointed sigh.

"Ugh, thank you. She rolled over on me during the night and refused to let go," Twinkaleni complains, straightening her fur.

Alice giggles, "Does that happen often?"

"Too often," the small mage assures.

Smiling, Alice looks out the window. The sky is still dark with the storm and it continues to rain, though not as heavily as it was the night before. The ever present winds have also become cooler with the abundant moisture.

"Looks like we're stayin' here for a while," says Alice, sticking her hand out to feel the rain only to retract it immediately when pain blooms in her elbow.

"If that is the case, we'll need to procure nourishment. How's your arm?" asks Twinkaleni, approaching to get a better look at it.

"It's alright," Alice lies.

"Mmm, perhaps you should rest. Danny and I will go look for something, perhaps the rain has-"

Danahlia's sneeze interrupts the mouse girl and the Liguna groans uncomfortably on the floor, "Ugh, guys?"

"We're here," Twinkaleni assures, the Tokala and Murin moving to check on the still prone girl.

"Can we get the fire goin'? It's freezin' in here," Danahlia moans, curling in on herself.

Alice and Twinkaleni share a look. True it was cool but hardly freezing. Twinkaleni kneels, placing a hand on Danahlia's forehead, "I don't feel a fever, but I suppose that isn't entirely irregular."

Danahlia sneezes again and then groans pitifully. Alice checks the ashes in the fireplace, the fire having died sometime during the night. They still have some warmth to them. With the persistent rains, any wood outside would be waterlogged by now so she looks around the small shack for anything that will burn. She spots a board hanging limply from the wall. In the past it may have served as a shelf but now she pries it off and tries to break it. She places the board against the wall at an angle and kicks down at it with a foot. After a few blows the board crackles into pieces.

Alice takes the smallest of these to the fireplace and blows at the ashes there. Her breath reveals a few glowing embers at the heart of the pile. She uses a splintered bit of wood to roll the embers into a tighter group and then sets some of the broken shelf over them. A few gentle breaths have the embers glowing bright as barely visible wisps of smoke begin to emerge from the wood. With a little more effort, she manages to get a small fire going and sits back to nurture it.

Meanwhile, Twinkaleni has been rummaging through their clothes only to come up with still damp garments. She takes those with the least moisture and gives them to Alice to dry, saying, "I'll go out to see if there is anything edible available in the immediate area."

"Not alone you're not, I'm go- ACHOO!" Danahlia sneezes, trying to rise.

Twinkaleni gently lays her back down, "No. You and Alice will stay here. Alice, look after her please."

"But I can-," Alice protests.

Twinkaleni interrupts with unusual sternness while dressing, "No. I need you to look after Danny. I won't be long."

"But," Alice starts again.

"I'll be fine. I'm not helpless you know," Twinkaleni says with a small smile as she dawns her backpack. The little mouse tries to open the door but it doesn't budge when she tugs at it. Alice leaves the fire to help. The wood of it must have soaked up some water because Alice has to put one foot on the wall and yank on the door knob with one hand as hard as she can before it swings open, the door nearly toppling over again. She catches it before it does and holds it open for the Murin.

Twinkaleni nods her thanks and then heads out into the rain. Alice watches her go, the mouse mage's large ears waving about as she immediately begins to search for anything useful. Another sneeze makes Alice jump.

"Why'd you let 'er go alone?" Danahlia groans weakly from where she stands hunched over behind the Tokala.

"She'll be fine, nothin's gonna to be out in this rain," Alice replies, looking after the mouse and hoping she's right. She closes the door most of the way, leaving it open just a bit in anticipation of Twinkaleni's return. Then, turning to the Liguna, she says, "You're sick and we need food."

Danahlia makes a feeble grunt, "I'm not-ACHOO!" The sneeze nearly topples the taller girl but Alice catches her as she groans, "It's just cold in here."

"You *are*, just rest for now," says Alice, noting the coolness of the Liguna's bare skin while leading her to the fire, setting her before it to warm up. Danahlia grumbles but doesn't move from where she's put.

Upon dressing and getting the fire to a respectable size, Alice busies herself by drying clothes, tossing the warmed garments over Danahlia, who has fallen back asleep. After perhaps half an hour, Alice checks out the window for any sign of Twinkaleni but doesn't spot the girl's gray fur anywhere. Sighing in worry she tests her hurt elbow, reminding herself that nothing dangerous should be about in the rain. Then she spots the window's shutter on the ground, weeds growing through the moldy old wood. Stomach on the sill and half hanging out in the rain, she picks it up, pulling off the other as well to set them over the fire. With the fire going already, she knows the shutters will dry and then burn too.

After settling back down to dry more clothes, Alice gets an idea. Just like when the rain started, she sets up her tent outside to capture water. Using the waterproof fabric along with a few sticks and rocks, she makes a little pool. Already wet, she decides to gather up some more fallen branches for the fire. She is doing this when she hears her name being called with some urgency. Immediately thinking of Twinkaleni, Alice searches the area, angling her ears to get a direction.

Spotting what appears to be the Murin's light coat some distance away among the darker browns and greens of local flora, Alice drops her bundle of sticks and starts to run, calling, "I see you! Hold on, I'm comin'!"

As she nears the mouse mage, she sees the Murin's steps are off like she's limping.

Alice doubles her pace shouting, "Are you alright?!"

Between haggard breaths, Twinkaleni says, "Fine. Just... fine."

Closer now, Alice can see the much smaller girl is working hard to drag something large and flat behind her. A few feet away now, Twinkaleni falls to her hands and knees in the mud trying desperately to catch her breath. Alice grabs her up in both arms, not caring at all about the cold, wet mud smearing onto her fur and clothes.

"I've been so worried. Are you ok? What happened?" she asks, looking over the little mouse to what may have been a feral once. It's mostly a rounded slab of gooey, red mush now.

"I'm fine, really. Just a bit winded is all," Twinkaleni assures, pushing lightly at the fox girl's embrace.

Alice squeezes the tiny Murin once more despite her resistance and then focuses on the mess behind her, "What was that?"

Twinkaleni takes in a deep breath before explaining, "Some sort of gargantuan amphibian. As I was foraging, this fellow began hopping after me. I ran for a time, but it just kept coming. Judging its intent to be ill, I threw a rock at it."

"A rock?" Alice asks, looking over the pulverized mass of soggy dirty flesh.

"A large rock," Twinkaleni replies defensively, "In any case, it perished. Thinking it a waste, I began trying to transport it back so we might gain some sustenance from its demise."

"Uh, ok," Alice says circling around the catch. Twinkaleni had been dragging it by two thickly muscled hind legs, though the rest, after being drawn through mud, leaves, sticks, and who knows what else, did not look appealing. "Let's head back, I'll get my sword and carve this guy up for us."

"Very well," Twinkaleni says in relief and the girls walk back toward the shack. As they do, Twinkaleni reveals that she's managed to find more of the chickenwood mushrooms and says there are even more among the trees.

Alice examines the cluster of fungi the Murin produces from her backpack, exclaiming, "Wow, good job! You slew a monster *and* got us food."

The little mouse beams at the compliment, using some of the water from the artificial pool to clean them off. Alice then enters the shack, shaking vigorously to dry off.

"Hey," Danahlia grumbles weakly, rising from under a pile of the girl's clothes while wiping drops of water from her face. Alice only grins, retrieving her sword, the Liguna wondering, "There anythin' to eat?"

"There will be, thanks to Twinkaleni," Alice replies happily, very proud of her tiny friend.

"She's back?"

"Mm-hm."

Danahlia sighs, "Good." This small exchange seems to use what little strength the lizard girl has, because she settles back down to the floor once more and closes her eyes.

Alice opens the door for the mouse mage, who asks, "How is she?"

"Better I think. She stopped sneezin' at least," replies the fox girl.

Twinkaleni slips by her, sets down her bundle of mushrooms, and then shakes much as Alice had, earning her a groan from Danahlia. Alice leaves the two, closing the door as much as the warped frame will allow, and heads off to where they left Twinkaleni's defeated foe. She finds it undisturbed and looks closely at it. Its skin would have served well to camouflage it among the trees and grasses, though it would get no benefit from it now, squished as it was. It may have looked very similarly to a frog or toad though much larger than any Alice had ever seen. It had similar legs anyhow. Deciding these where all that could be salvaged, Alice hacks them off near its hip to get the most out of its thick thighs. They're a good weight and assuming the legs are as meaty as they look, Alice figures they might last the trio a day or even two. Leaving the rest, the young fox carries these over her shoulder and back to her friends, trying to keep from straining her right elbow.

As Alice nears the shack, she hears Twinkaleni recounting her foraging adventure in length and uninterrupted, which makes her think Danahlia might be sleeping again. She cleans off the legs in the tent pool and finds the dark brown and green mottled skin peeling away rather easily. She strips both legs to find the muscle beneath is a healthy pink.

"Oh, it's Alice," Twinkaleni says, poking her head out the window.

Danahlia opens the door, "Mmm, those look good."

Alice grins, "You're up, feelin' better?"

"Eh, Twinkie's been going on and on about how she took out somethin' out there. Hard to rest with all that. Those legs?"

"Yeah. How'd you wanna cook'em?"

"Twinkie already has the pot going with the mushrooms, let's put 'em in there like yesterday."

Danahlia settles back down by the fire, wrapped in loose clothes, while Twinkaleni cleans off the small wooden table with some damp rags.

Alice plops the legs down atop it and, with their giant ant mandibles, the girls separate the muscle from the bone. Once done, Alice uses her sword to cut a thigh into chunks to be placed into the crab shell bowl, already steaming with its contents of water and mushrooms.

She isn't worried about cleaning the weapon. Ever since the pixies of her home forest enchanted the simple broadsword, she hadn't had to. Whenever it got dirty now, the blade would glow with an intense but heatless green light which would turn whatever tarnished it into fine ash. This would then flake away, leaving the blade looking freshly polished. Jellybane does this now and no matter how many times she sees it, it is still an impressive display of magical power.

The two wash up and then let the dirty water from the tent drain to be replaced with more before joining Danahlia in waiting for their meal. Alice sees the fire is getting low, reminding her of the branches she was collecting earlier. Not entirely eager to get soaked again after just starting to get dry, she puts on Danahlia's cloak before heading back out. Twinkaleni offers to come but Alice insists she stay, knowing it will only take a minute.

She locates the pile of dropped sticks easily enough. Gathering them back up, she finds her right arm is feeling more able to contribute to the task. Encouraged by this, she wanders around picking up more bits of potential fire wood, the heavy rains and wind having knocked down plenty of branches. As she does, Alice is reminded of how the rain would be bringing out the jellies back in Toki village. On that thought, she wonders who would be dealing with them now. As always when reminded of home, the young Tokala's thoughts turn to her friend, Ashleigh, and her mother. She wonders how the Didels are doing and if they ever think of her. She amuses herself with the idea of Ashleigh taking up where Alice left off as the local monster hunter, battling jellies and collecting cores for her mother's shop, just like she always wanted.

Lost in these thoughts, Alice doesn't notice that the rain is getting steadily stronger until a loud rumble of thunder rolls overhead, snapping her back. She's wandered a little further than she meant to and hurries back to the shack. Twinkaleni is looking out the one window and disappears when she spots Alice. The fox jogs to the door with her load of sticks needing to keep her head down because the hood of the cloak has flown back. When she nears the door, it opens and she patters in.

Danahlia, Twinkaleni, and the scent of warm food greet her. The girls hadn't eaten all day and now, well into the afternoon, they are ravenous. Danahlia accepts the bundle of branches and drops them beside the fireplace. She then breaks a few pieces of the damp wood to place into the fire.

"How's the soup comin'?" Alice asks eagerly.

"Think it's done," Danahlia replies happily.

Alice uses the wet cloak to pull the hot crab shell bowl from the fire before taking it off. She takes in a deep breath through the nostrils, the soup smelling wonderfully of the mushrooms.

"The rain is becoming stronger again," Twinkaleni says dismally, once more by the window. As if to agree, the storm unleashes a flash of lightning followed closely by the rumble of thunder, causing the mouse mage to retreat to her companions around the steaming bowl of soup.

In between blows over their meal, Alice says, "No worries. We're safe in here. We'll just wait it out."

"Yeah," Danahlia agrees, patting a place on the ground beside her.

Twinkaleni sits with them musing, "I'm more concerned about our pursuer from the Order of Thermathrogi. The longer we linger in any one spot, the closer I fear they will become."

Hearing her say this makes Alice worry a bit too. The girls know next to nothing of the individual who hunts them now, other than they desire to take Twinkaleni back to that horrible school, or perhaps even kill her for escaping.

"Relax. They probably aren't even half way through the pixie forest yet," Danahlia assures.

Alice nods, "Plus, if the rain is slowin' us down, it's got to be doin' the same to them."

"I do hope you're right," says Twinkaleni, rubbing her tiny hands together nervously.

"How long are we gonna have 'em on our tail anyway? We're not gonna to be on the run forever are we?" asks Danahlia, touching the bowl and finding it still too hot to handle.

"No, no, not forever… I don't think," the little mage says uncertainly.

"Don't think?" Alice asks, her brows rising and ears perking up.

"Well, I don't possess any experience using tracking spells myself, but from what I've read, it seems very unlikely that such magic could last indefinitely."

"How unlikely?" wonders Danahlia.

Twinkaleni thinks for a moment, "Highly, almost entirely."

"Why is that?" inquires Alice before putting her face near the bowl to feel the heat radiating off from it.

"Mmm, that has to do with how tracking magic works," Twinkaleni starts, "As I've mentioned before, the only way they can be tracking me now is by using my tail. This is only possible because my tail was once a part of me."

Both larger girls look to the Murin curiously, Danahlia commenting, "So?"

"So," Twinkaleni continues, "My tail was part of me, one part of a whole. It belonged to me. Such a sense of belonging creates a connection. Such things can occur with almost anything that is cared for over time. This connection is especially strong since it was once a physical part of me, something I was born with and still feel a yearning for." She reaches behind herself to touch the little bare nub that's left before going on, "There are ways of tapping into such connections and following them to their source."

"But your tail will always belong to you. Doesn't that mean they'll just keep bein' able to use it to find us?" Alice asks, images of some menacing stranger holding up Twinkaleni's severed tail as it twitches in response to the mage's presence popping into the young fox's head.

"I don't believe so. Fortunately, we are living beings. As such, we change throughout our lives. We grow, we learn, and we adapt."

"How does that help?" Danahlia asks, in between blows over the soup.

"Well, when my tail was cut off, I was a bit younger, afraid, running for my life, uncertain of anything, and knew little of the world. That is the

Twinkaleni the tail belonged to when it was removed. I've changed since then. I've grown..." she notices Alice grinning at her and amends, "... perhaps not significantly in stature, but I have adapted to the loss, gained new experiences, learned and tried new things-"

"Made new friends," Alice adds.

The little mage smiles, "Indeed, and all this has pushed me little by little from the Twinkaleni I once was. Slowly, as I continue to change and grow as an individual, the connection between my lost tail and I should weaken. Eventually, it will become too weak to be traced and then I will finally be free of the Order."

"About how long does that usually take?" Danahlia asks, picking out a floating bit of meat and popping it into her mouth.

"I'm not sure, changing who you are takes time. But my tail is undoubtedly changing as well, slowly decaying naturally. Though I suspect the agent sent after me would be slowing the process further with some preservation techniques," Twinkaleni finishes scornfully.

"So we just have to keep ahead of 'em until they can't use that connection to find you anymore," Alice announces.

"Sounds do-able," Danahlia nods and takes a sip from the bowl.

The girls then pass the bowl around, taking turns drinking from it. The mushrooms have flavored the soup well, and the warmth of it is a great comfort in their empty bellies. They quickly finish it off and then use their fingers to eat the bits of meat and mushroom left at the bottom. It's a nice meal anywhere, made all the better shared. The girls eat their fill as the storm outside rages on.

Flashes of lighting and crashes of thunder are becoming more frequent as the rain hammers the small shack's roof. Alice decides to cook the rest of the meat before the water pouring in through the chimney douses their fire. Danahlia curls back up under a blanket of clothes while Twinkaleni watches the storm strengthen. Several deafening cracks of thunder have the little mouse scurrying between Alice and Danahlia, holding her ears folded against her head as she trembles.

Danahlia sits up and takes the smaller girl in her arms, "Calm down, we're safe in here."

As if to challenge this, the shack creaks noisily under the relentless storm. The girls look up and around nervously, cool drops of rain blowing in through the window, while the roof leaks more readily. Alice refocuses on her efforts, having to put their crab shell bowl upside down over the fire to protect it from the intruding water trying to put it out. Setting the still mostly raw meat directly on the charred wood, Alice places a few more damp sticks about it, hoping what's left of the fire will help dry them.

The water dripping from the chimney begins to pool in the fireplace, threatening the heart of the small fire itself. Alice decides to change tactics and uses a branch to scoop up the burning bits of wood, with the still cooking meat, into the crab shell bowl. She carries the bowl over to where Twinkaleni and Danahlia are huddled together in a dry spot on the floor. She nearly drops it when another monstrous crash of thunder makes her jump, the ground shuddering under her feet. Twinkaleni hides her face in Danahlia side, the lizard girl raising an arm to Alice.

She joins them, setting the bowl beside her so she can nurture the struggling flame within. As she does, Danahlia starts to sing softly to the frightened mouse girl. Alice is surprised to hear that it's a song her mother used to sing, long ago.

Even on these nights, when we're faaar apaart.
I can feel you, in my heart.

In all my dreams, you're so veeery neear.
When I wake, you're not here.

Though the wind blows, and the raaain may faall.
I'll be waiting, through it all.

I know one day, you'll come baaack to mee.
Then together, again we'll be.

'til then I'll wait, I'll wait eeevery daay.
And every night, I will pray.

Good-bye feels like, like so looong agoo,
Count the days, so I know.

Seasons change, and the yeeears go byy.
So many nights, alone I cry.

After a few lyrics Alice joins in the sad little song and Danahlia gives her a squeeze with one arm. As the storm outside batters their little shack, water begins to pool under the door as puddles reach out from the fire place and other leaks. They sing other songs, getting louder with each crash of thunder, trying to drown out the worst of it. Twinkaleni seems comforted by what someone passing outside might only call rhythmic shouting, but it helps pass the time.

That night, Alice is sitting in her old house in Toki village. Cradling her head in both hands, elbows on the table, she watches the dancing flame of a candle set out to guide her father home. She listens to her mother's singing, though at the time she paid little attention to the words, only knowing they sounded beautiful coming from her. Alice doesn't look, but knows, as one does in their dreams, that her mother is sitting nearby, stitching up a hole in one of her old skirts.

"When's daddy comin' home?" Alice asks, as she often did then.

Her mother offers the reply she always would with a smile in her tone, "I don't know, little kit, maybe tonight. We just have to keep watching for 'im."

The dream changes then, and Alice is seeing her younger self staring into the candle by the window. They set one out every night with the hope that should her father arrive in the village late, he would easily find his way back to them. The little fox wags her tail while rocking her head slowly back and forth to her mother's tune, the flickering flame before her eyes. She had taken to sleeping on the floor beside the door, her blanket laid out just beside it, that way she'd know the instant he was back.

Alice knows her father won't be coming home but she watches the candle, letting her younger self hope for as long as she can.

Chapter 4

The Muck

Alice awakes to Danahlia sucking on her ear. She starts, bumping the larger girl's chin, waking her up too.

"Agh, uh? Ugh, gross!" Alice exclaims, feeling the warm moisture left on the very tip of her right ear.

"Wha, what's wrong with you?" grumbles Danahlia, shimming back under some clothes.

"You had my ear, in your mouth!" Alice complains, using someone's shirt sleeve to wipe the slobber away.

Danahlia scrapes her tongue over her upper lip, "Ugh, I thought that dream tasted fuzzy."

Twinkaleni, awakened by the commotion, wiggles free from under Danahlia's other arm and scampers over to the window to announce, "The sky has finally cleared!"

Alice gets up, walking over damp floor boards, to open the door. Water still drips readily off every exposed surface but the clouds have all moved on, making way for the shining sun. Alice takes a deep breath, enjoying the freshness of the damp air.

"Guess that means we can finally get movin'," says Danahlia.

"Yes, at last we can- ugh, Danny, some modesty, please," says Twinkaleni, turning only to avert her gaze.

Alice looks over to find Danahlia, who's risen from the pile of clothes completely nude. She laughs and looks away as Danahlia stretches, "You guys are too bashful."

The girls pack there things and Danahlia dresses, eventually. Alice finds the leg meat left in the crab shell bowl has been smoked fairly well, and with a little scraping, doesn't taste half bad. On their way out, Danahlia gives the weathered shack's door frame a pat, saying, "Thanks for protecting us from the storm and junk."

The path they took to the shack has been entirely washed away but Twinkaleni suggests they try to reacquire it, thinking if this end led to the shack then the other end must lead to a larger path or even a village.

"If we can find a settlement of some kind, we'll be able to get an idea of where we are, perhaps even acquire a map," the little mouse bubbles, clearly very pleased to be on the road again.

"Yer, gat hounds goth," agrees Alice, munching on some of the dry, smoked meat.

Danahlia swallows a mouthful herself and gives the bit left in her hand a shake, "You did good takin' this thing down for us, Twinkie. Maybe we can bag another one before we get too far." The Murin grins widely and starts to nibble on her own breakfast.

Mud squishes under their feet, and the girls soon make a little game of hopping to the driest patches of earth they can find. As they hop along, Alice picks up a strange noise, a sort of high pitched hum just on the edge of her hearing.

Danahlia lands nearby and Alice gently tugs on her tail, "You guys hear that?"

"Hear what?" the Liguna asks, looking around for her next dryish patch.

Twinkaleni comes to a stop, tilting her head to listen, "That humming sound?"

"Yeah, what is that?" wonders Alice, her ears angling in different direction, trying to find where it's coming from.

"I don't hear anythin'," says Danahlia, preparing her next hop.

Alice tugs again on her tail, stilling the taller girl. The hum seems to be coming from everywhere, though looking around she doesn't see a source, only dripping trees and muddy grass.

The girls move on, walking now while listening for any change in the subtle sound that might indicate danger. Danahlia hears it too but is distracted by the discovery of more chickenwood mushrooms growing at the base of an old tree. They gather the lot, Alice and Twinkaleni looking around cautiously, while the lizard girl crams the fungi into their packs. Now standing still, Alice notices the buzzing is joined by a sporadic plopping. The girls own sloshing through the mud must have masked it before, for it sounds fairly close by.

"I believe that may be another of those massive creatures I slew before. Though I don't recall all this buzzing," informs Twinkaleni.

Danahlia scans around, putting the last of the mushrooms into Alice's backpack, "Good, we could use the meat. Make some more soup or somethin'."

"Wanna go hunt it? Maybe we can find out what's making that hum," Alice suggests, curious about the sounds.

The trio decides to make a short detour, following the plopping noises to their source. Both the hum and the wet little splashes get louder as they near their quarry. The puddles are larger and more frequent in the new direction, becoming unavoidable. Twinkaleni holds her baggy pant legs up, but their bottoms are still getting muddy. Grimacing as she plods behind the taller girls she suggests they head back and seek food in dryer locals.

Danahlia dismisses the little mage, claiming she sees something up ahead. Through the trees, Alice can see the source too, or sources of the noise. Things that look vaguely like giant toads are hopping madly around in the shallow muddy water. Their mottled skin blends in well with their now swampy wooded surroundings as they leap about on large hind legs, just like the ones the girls had eaten. Bulbous yellow eyes peer about from under thick rough looking brows, but most impressive are their mouths. The creatures' jaws are significantly larger than the toads Alice is familiar with. The edges of them curve up, giving them the impression that they are grinning rather sinisterly whenever their mouths are shut.

When open, a long fleshy pink tongue would often come lashing out at what looks to be giant mosquitoes. The beating of their wings is clearly the source of the high pitched hum as its loudest now. The insects must be at least as long as Alice's arm, sporting a proboscis nearly as long. The toad monsters are feasting on the mosquitoes, hitting them with their apparently sticky tongues and bringing them back to engulf the bugs with their abnormally large jaws. Strangely, the mosquitoes seem drawn to the toads despite this. The girls soon see why.

While eating a giant mosquito, one of the toads is surrounded by several more of the flying stick-limbed insects. Landing, they stick their straw like probes into the toad's back and after only a short while, the toad begins to deflate as if its insides were being sucked right out of it. Then, as the toad withers away, its eyes dissolve in wisps of smoke. Once the toad is only a skeletal husk the mosquitoes move on.

"Ticks and fleas! Did you see that? They just sucked that thing dry," Danahlia exclaims, pointing with her spear.

"Danny! Not so loud, they may hear us," Twinkaleni whispers harshly.

"We, we need to get outta here before they do that to us," Alice whispers, trying to keep calm.

In agreement, the girls start to sneak away. By this time, it seems the whole area has been engulfed in this bizarre battle. Giant mosquitoes buzz around getting eaten by toads, while some toads, and various other creatures, are literally drained of their life. Alice and Danahlia hand their packs to Twinkaleni so they may fight without hindrance, both readying their weapons. The girls try to avoid them but occasionally a mosquito will take interest. The insects seem unafraid or perhaps unaware of what the girls are capable of and the trio leaves a trail of dead bugs in their wake.

Alice and Danahlia stay close to Twinkaleni, guarding their little pack mouse as they try to find a way out of this mess. Fortunately, the mosquitoes' approach is very audible, which keeps the insects from surprising the girls, though even trying to avoid them, the frequency of encounters steadily increases. Alice cuts through wings and part of a body only to see another flying towards them in awkward, short swoops. The trees are hampering the insects, preventing them from gaining much altitude, which aids the girls in dispatching them. Lashing toad tongues frequently rip a mosquito from the air, but as the three press on, Alice notices the toads' numbers dwindling while the mosquitoes persist.

"Geez, they're freaking everywhere," grumbles Danahlia, beating a plump mosquito to the ground before piercing its body with the tip of her spear. Whatever poor creature it slurped up comes oozing out with a puff of steam. "Ugh, gross. Watch your feet," the Liguna warns.

The smell of whatever the massive insects inject into their prey to liquefy their insides is acrid and intensely so, making Alice's nostrils burn and eyes water. She hears another mosquito's high pitched wings coming close and through blurred vision she slashes upward, taking off a wing and a few limbs. The giant bug falls to the mud, stick like legs waving frantically as it fails to regain its footing.

As Alice turns back toward her companions, something warm and wet, slaps her ankle. She looks to see a fleshy pink tongue extending several yards away to a toad that hops eagerly toward her, grinning mouth open wide. Fortunately, the toad doesn't have a very good hold and Alice manages to pull away, but the tongue is so sticky that it tears a bit of fur off as it snaps back to its owner, making her cry out. The toad is quickly distracted by the swarming mosquitoes letting the girls hurry away.

They stumble on for some time, quickly becoming exhausted from having to fend off attack after attack. The mosquitoes are relentless and the toads are dangerous allies at best. Danahlia leads with Twinkaleni following while Alice covers the rear. Alice's sword, Jellybane, glows frequently to shed the various vital fluids that attempt to stain it. Even enchanted, the sword is still heavy and costs Alice precious stamina with each swing. Her breathing is rapid, arms tired, and lungs burn but she shambles on, her friends looking no better.

She nearly trips over Twinkaleni when the mouse girl falls face first into the mud. The backpacks she holds tumble from her grasp as she is immediately jerked away several feet by another toad's elastic tongue. The mage burbles and flails, the tongue having taken hold of one of her small bare feet.

"Twinkaleni!" cries Alice, using what little she has left to charge after the small girl as she is reeled in by the hungry monster. Danahlia turns in time to see Alice dash between the toad and its potential meal, coming down hard with a mud splashing chop that severs the toad's tongue. Alice rips off the fleshy pink bit stuck to Twinkaleni's foot, and then helps the Murin to her feet.

Danahlia takes the little mouse by the hand and pulls the sputtering girl along, calling, "Come on, we gotta go!"

Twinkaleni spits enough mud from her mouth to shout, "The packs!"

Alice turns to where the mouse girl had dropped the others' backpacks, but several mosquitoes are already too close to get to them safely. The Tokala gauges her remaining strength and how much she would need to dispatch the insects, take up the bags, and rejoin her companions before more arrive.

She's about to make her move when Danahlia shouts back to her, "Leave 'em! We gotta get outta here!"

Alice is about to try anyway but then notices more mosquitoes have already come and are attacking the tongue-less toad. It manages to hop at one, grabbing it in its mouth before the others pierce it with their proboscises. Watching this, she loses her chance and Danahlia shouts from further away, "Forget 'em, we need to go NOW!"

The girls limp along fending off more attackers, though their numbers steadily drop as the swampy forest gives way to more open country. A few of the hostile bugs managed to penetrate Alice's defenses and have left a handful of shallow stab wounds from where they tried to stick their sharp, rapier-like mouths into her. Danahlia has collected her share too, winding trails of blood running down her arms.

The Liguna turns around to scan for pursuers. Not finding any, she finally calls for a break. The trio collapses in to the damp grass, taking a moment to drink from their waterskins, assess wounds, and catch their breath. No one is badly hurt, but they did lose much of their supplies, mostly clothes, but also Alice's tent, bow, and shoulder bag, all their arrows, the crab shell bowl, and the core stones the two packs held.

As soon as she is able to speak, Twinkaleni gasps, "I'm... I'm sorry... I'm sorry."

Alice checks her ankle to find a small patch of black fur missing, the flesh underneath an angry red, "Don't pant it, it was just stuff. How's your foot?"

"Yeah, we can always get more," says Danahlia, distastefully wiping up a bit of her blood still oozing from a small puncture in her arm.

"I should... I should have, held onto them..." the little mouse goes on from where she lies on her back.

Alice crawls over to her and examines the foot the toad's tongue had stuck onto. Some of the skin has been removed and it looks dirty and painful, though Twinkaleni doesn't react to it. With a little water and a relatively clean bit of her blouse sleeve, Alice wipes away the mud around the wound. Twinkaleni twitches a little but otherwise stays still.

"It's ok, we can trade for more supplies in the next village. We still have your core stones," assures Alice.

Danahlia rolls the mouse girl to her side and removes one of the oversized shirts from her pack. The Liguna then begins tearing the garment into strips to be used as bandages. The girls patch themselves up and lay about for some much needed rest.

It's well into the afternoon when Danahlia, fiddling with the white fluff at the end of Alice's tail, asks, "Well, what should we do now?"

Alice looks to Twinkaleni, who has fallen asleep, her own movements feeling sluggish, "I think we need to find a village to get some supplies and rest. It's too dangerous out here in the open."

Danahlia sighs, but agrees. A village meant people, and people increased the chances of Danahlia's Liguna features being discovered, plus word of their passing might reach whoever was sent by the Order to find Twinkaleni. But now, hurt, tired, and low on supplies, their options were few. Danahlia crawls over to Twinkaleni. She then gently strokes her fur until the little Murin wakes.

Twinkaleni blinks sleep from her eyes, "Oh, I, I must have dosed off."

Danahlia smiles, "Yeah, you ready to get movin'?"

"Uh, yes, yes of course." As the little mouse girl rises and hikes up her back pack, she wonders, "Do we have a plan?"

"We need to find a village or somethin' to restock our supplies," answers Alice, adjusting the sword on her back.

"Right, so, the same plan we had this morning?"

"Yup, minus the monsters," Alice grins.

"Very well, which direction shall we wander in?" asks Twinkaleni, looking around.

"I got a good feelin' about thataway," announces Danahlia, pointing roughly northeast.

The girls walk for a few hours, the sparse trees giving way to flat grassy plains, and eventually find a road. This one is well defined and looks recently traveled, unlike the small path to the shack.

Danahlia conceals herself the best she can under her cloak, grinning, "See I knew this was a good direction."

Spirits up, they follow the road to wherever it may lead.

By evening, the trio can see a small town in the distance and as they near, the tiny light of candles can be seen in several windows. They travel off road for some time and into a crop of oak trees where Danahlia can keep hidden.

"We can probably fill up on water, but any shops are gonna be closed by now," says Alice, looking over the huddle of buildings.

Twinkleni takes a drink, "Indeed. The darkness will, however, be an excellent cover to search the town for those who may be willing to aid us. Danny, we cannot afford another incident like last time, you *must* stay hidden."

"I know, I know, geez, shed it already," the Liguna says, handing Alice her empty waterskins.

Danahlia then climbs one of the thicker oaks and, in the growing darkness, disappears into the branches. After back tracking to the road to help avoid suspicion, Alice and Twinkaleni head into town.

The moon has risen by the time they arrive on the outskirts. Fields for growing crops surround the town and look well-tended to. Few are still out and about though the sounds of the residence can occasionally be heard settling in for the night. The buildings here are largely composed of wood, just as the ones in Alice's village, though there are a few made of mud brick, and even some burrows dug into mounds.

Alice feels like an intruder, skulking around in the night within these unfamiliar surroundings. She whispers, "What should we look for first? A shop or a well?"

When her question goes unanswered, she looks to find herself alone in the middle of a main road. Looking back, she spots Twinkaleni a few houses away feeling around a fence post with a small gate leading into someone's front garden.

Alice makes her way over to the Murin, "What're you doin'?"

"Looking for the marks," she replies, feeling low on the fence post, particularly the back side facing the house. Not finding what she is looking for, she hurries on to another post before a different house.

Alice follows along, confused, "What marks?"

"It's a sort of code developed to aid refugees," she whispers, moving on to another.

Twinkleni explains while scampering from house to house, "Considering the long peace before the war, many do not harbor ill will toward the Cold Bloods. Few even lend aid when they can, despite the harsh penalties. Refugees, like Danny, have created a simple code to help others of their kind find these people when they are in need."

Alice crouches by Twinkaleni, "Are there lots of refugees?"

"Of course, some thousands were likely cut off from their homelands when the war broke out. Many travel in secret trying to avoid capture, just as we are."

"What does that have to do with touching fence posts?"

"I'll, oh, here, feel this," says Twinkaleni, gesturing for Alice's hand. Alice holds one out to her and the little mouse girl places it on the back side of the fence post, just above the ground. "Feel those?"

Alice feels around with her fingers where Twinkaleni guides her but aside from some scratches she doesn't feel anything unusual, "No, what?"

Twinkanleni guides her fingers with her own, "Those scratch marks."

"Uh, yeah, I feel those. Is that what you've been looking for?"

"Yes, two scratches and one dot. We found one," Twinkaleni whispers excitedly.

Alice moves her fingers around and can feel two horizontal scratches parallel to each other, maybe an inch long, and a tiny dip just under them like someone stabbed at the wood.

"What do they mean? Found what?" asks a curious Alice.

"It means we can go get Danny, come on," says Twinkaleni, grabbing Alice by the wrist to pull her back the way they came.

Alice trails the eager mage, staying low, back to the crop of trees where Danahlia is waiting. Once they're out in the grassy field, she asks, "The marks mean that house is safe?"

Without turning to her, Twinkaleni answers, "In all probability, yes, but we must still be cautious. Just because one house offers safety, doesn't mean the neighbors do as well, and we mustn't attract undo attention to those who would offer us respite."

Navigating by starlight, the two approach the cluster of oaks and call for Danahlia.

"Yeah, I'm here. That was fast, find anything good?" she calls from above.

"We found a sympathizer, two talons and a tooth," answers Twinkaleni.

Alice looks to the Murin, "We, what?"

Danahlia swings down to land beside them, "Wags, let's go."

The trio heads back to the house, Alice repeating, "Two talons and a tooth?"

"Oh yes, the marks. A talon is a scratch and a tooth is a dot. It's often wise to refer to them in code encase anyone is listening," says Twinkaleni.

"What do they mean?"

This time Danahlia answers, "It's a check list. Top mark is food, middle is shelter, bottom one is danger. If the top mark is a talon that means the people in that house might have food. If the middle one is scratched that means they may let you stay and rest for a little while. But if the bottom one is scratched that means the house and probably the rest of the town is bad."

"Indeed. Ours is a fortunate find. Two talons means they may offer us food and shelter," Twinkaleni adds.

The girls quiet down as they near the town, not wanting to alert anyone to their presence. Though the other two seem confident, Alice remains uncertain and cautious. In her experience, it was very rare that people gave without wanting something in return. When they approach the house, Danahlia feels for the marks too and nods her approval. A candle is lit in one of the windows but other than that the house is dark, as are most on the street.

They quietly open and close the short gate, a wooden fence extending from it and around the house, standing guard over a lovingly tended garden. The trio then follows a few stepping stones to the front door. The house isn't large but is definitely more than one room. Danahlia under her cloak, raps on the door a few times with a claw before looking away. After a few moments, Alice spots the shifting of a shadow by the candle light in the window. The candle then vanishes and after a few seconds more, a woman's voice calls through the door, "Yes?"

"Good evening madam, the moon is shining brightly tonight," says Twinkaleni and Alice looks at her, confused.

"Oh, and the luna lilly will bloom again at midnight," the woman replies as the door opens a few inches. The head that pokes out is that of a Lotarin in her middle years. The raccoon woman's black nose wiggles as she sniffs, white whiskers shifting on either side of her white furred muzzle. Black patches extend from her cheeks up to surprised, brown eyes. Her raised brows are white and fade into the dominate gray of her coat. "Why, you're only children."

"Yes. We seek refuge from the night, if you have any room to spare," says Twinkaleni.

Danahlia keeps silent but turns her head to the woman while Alice, unfamiliar with the situation, let's her companion do the talking.

The woman sees Danahlia and nods, "Of course, of course, come on in, hurry now."

The door opens fully and she ushers the girls inside, looking back along the road before closing the door behind them. Once in, the girls thank the rather squat, kindly woman for letting them into her home at such an hour. She shakes her head and gestures for them to follow her. She has a thick, ringed tail poking free from the back of a light blue night gown that covers most of her figure. The candle she carries only dimly lights the immediate area, covering the rest of the house in shadow.

The girls follow the woman in silence until she leads them to what looks to be the kitchen/dining area. Placing the candle on a counter top, the Lotarin woman pulls away a rug from the hardwood floor and then paws around as if feeling for something. Alice looks to her companions who simply wait patiently, so she does too.

The woman takes hold of something in the floor and pulls up to reveal a trap door concealing a stairway of packed earth. She then hands Danahlia the candle and gestures for them to go down, "Make yourselves at home, I'll be with you in two shakes."

Danahlia thanks the woman again and gets a smile before she hurries them below.

Alice follows her friends, noting how much cooler the air is underground. The candle light is obscured by Danahlia's body, but she can smell the dirt around them and reaches out to her sides to feel the earthen walls. After only a few steps, the girls come to a small chamber that must have once been the house's cellar, though now it has four old bedrolls on the floor in a loose circle around an end table. A thick, well used candle is on one corner of the table in a puddle of wax. Danahlia lights it.

"We can stay here?" asks Alice, breaking the silence.

"For a little while," answers Danahlia, setting down her spear and bow against a wall.

Twinkaleni removes her pack to let it rest against a table leg with a relieved sigh, she then begins rummaging through it. Alice looks around, finding a few vegetables hanging from twine along the inside of shelves carved from the earth. Seeing some garlic, potatoes, and carrots, Alice's stomach growls, reminding her they hadn't eaten since this morning. She's about to ask if they can eat the vegetables when the sounds of movement, back the way they had come, alerts them to the raccoon woman reappearing with a tray laden with a large bowl of something steaming, three spoons, and another lit candle.

"It's not much, but it'll get you through the night," she says, setting the tray on the table.

Twinkaleni approaches the woman and holds out three core stones of various colors, "For your trouble."

"Oh, those are beautiful," the woman says, peering down at them.

"You can trade them, they're worth quite a bit," informs Alice.

The woman smiles picking only one, the blue core, saying, "Blue's my favorite color." She then closes Twinkaleni's fingers over the others, "You hold onto those." With that, she looks over the girls in the greater light of the candles and shakes her head solemnly, "Goodness, you're all so young, and where did you get all those- never mind, never mind that now. Go on and eat before it gets cold. I'll see about changing those bandages." She lingers a moment more as the girls gather around the table before retreating back upstairs.

"What'd ya think?" asks Danahlia, picking up a wooden spoon and stirring what turns out to be a thin vegetable soup.

"She seems nice," says Alice, joining in.

Twinkaleni replaces the core stones before sniffing the soup, "Indeed. And a town of this size should have a few shops where we can trade.

"You guys did this kinda thing before, right?" Alice asks, looking around.

"Sure, lots o' times," Danahlia replies.

"If not for the sympathy people, such as our host, have for the plight of trapped refugees, we undoubtedly would not have lasted as long as we have," admits Twinkaleni, bringing a spoon to her mouth.

Twinkaleni goes on in length about various other times Danahlia and she had stayed with other sympathizers as the girls drink the soup, letting the warmth of it settle their rumbling bellies. Danahlia often interrupts the Murin to add her own colorful commentary and Alice listens, thinking how different her life has become since meeting these two, how fluid. Life back in Toki was uncertain but the tasks from day to day were fairly similar to each other. Now though, everyday seemed its own adventure.

The kind Lotarin returns with another large bowl, this one of plain water, and a modest stack of torn rags just as the girls finish the soup. The three thank her and she smiles, introducing herself as Anna Ringtail, while exchanging the empty soup bowl for the one filled with water. Alice and her friends introduce themselves in return as she sits beside Alice and starts to untie one of the bandages on her arm, saying, "You girls look like you've been on the road for a while now. Why not wash up a bit and we'll get these wounds checked."

Twinkaleni and Danahlia grab a rag each, dunk it in the water and begin cleaning themselves. They've all accumulated an unappealing amount of grime in their recent travels and eagerly scrub it off. The puncture wounds they received from the abnormally large mosquitoes have stopped bleeding but still look unpleasant.

Alice twitches uncomfortably as Ms. Ringtail removes the bandage, sticky with partially dried blood, asking, "Are you girl's traveling alone? Where are your mothers?"

The other two hesitate, so Alice answers, "We haven't any."

"Oh, oh I'm so sorry dear. I don't mean to pry. It's just been a while since I've had visitors. The last was a young Iguna man, a bit older than you dear," the raccoon woman says to Danahlia, "That was well over a month ago now. He didn't talk much or stay long, but he was a polite one."

Ms. Ringtail goes on about previous visitors, seemingly very eager to talk, while the girls do their best to clean up. After a few minutes she is looking curiously at a couple of the puncture wounds on Alice's body, "Now these remind me of the bites from those monstrous culicades. You girls didn't come from the southern muck did you?"

"We did travel here from the southwest," offers Twinkaleni.

"Oh goodness, then these *are* from those awful insects. You girls are lucky to be alive. Everyone 'round Carton knows not to be out in the muck after a good rain-"

"Carton, is that the name of this town?" asks Danahlia.

"Why yes, yes it is," Ms. Ringtail acknowledges, redressing Alice's arm, "Lucky for us those nasty things don't last. Pop up only long enough to be a bother to anyone not bein' careful, lay their eggs, and then, thankfully, die. Was a time before all this bloody war nonsense when folk would head into the muck and gather up their eggs, used to be somethin' to look forward to. My momma made the best culicades omelets in town, you ask anyone. Course, these days, with so many gone, there're just too many dangers out there now."

Ms. Ringtail goes on about better times and asks the girls a bit about themselves. Alice notices

Danahlia and Twinkaleni are hesitant to answer questions fully and takes the cue to do so as well.

Out of nowhere, a strange feeling overwhelms the young Tokala while Ms. Ringtail is tying another new bandage over her shoulder. Tidal waves of nostalgia and grief have her vision blurring as she recalls times when her mother used to fuse over her whenever she got a cut or scrapped her knee when she was a kit. She tries desperately to force the intense feelings aside, shaking her head as if it might make the thoughts tumble out, but a tear rolls down her cheek instead.

"Oh, I'm so sorry, dear, was that one too tight? Here, let me loosen it," Ms. Ringtail offers taking hold of the cloth again.

Alice pulls away an inch, sniffing, "No, it's fine, thank you," and looks to the ground, more tears falling.

She burns with embarrassment, unable to face the others' gazes, as she frantically wipes her eyes. Suddenly, Danahlia is beside her, pulling Alice gently into her chest.

Cradling her head, the older girl whispers into her ear, "I know." Alice tries to pull away but

Danahlia holds her tighter, repeating the words again and again.

Somewhere inside the young fox, a weathered dam finally breaks and she begins to cry.

The lost hope after she had heard of her father's death. The slow torture as she watched her mother slip away, and the feeling of abandonment after. Seeing her house after she was told she couldn't live there anymore. The times she'd stood alone after the other children were called home to dinner. The scrapes and cuts she had to patch herself. The long limps back to her hill after a nasty fall. The days of uncertainty when she wandered on an empty stomach, not knowing when or from where her next meal might come, and the hollowness that lingered even after she could eat. The late evenings she lay with no one to tuck her in. The dark nights when she had bad dreams and could only wait for dawn.

She thought these struggles had made her stronger. Stronger than the kids who still had at least one parent to rely on, who still had homes to go back to, and had someone to assure them that they were loved. To cry now would be to admit it was all a lie. To cry now would be to admit that she was just as weak and frightened as she had always been. But she just can't force it back any more.

To burden someone else with her weakness makes Alice feel horribly ashamed even as she bawls in Danahlia's arms. Danahlia had lost her parents too, and Twinkaleni never even got to know hers. They didn't cry. How could she be so weak, so frail, after all she endured? It makes her furious with herself, until she feels moisture dripping atop her head, just before Danahlia's damp chin comes to rest between her ears. As the two share their wordless pain, Twinkaleni offers a small hand on both their arms, though the youngest of the group only stands in silence.

An unknown time later, Alice feels completely flushed out and exhausted. Ms. Ringtail has long since left them and Twinkaleni is already asleep atop one of the bed rolls. Danahlia pulls away and Alice immediately misses her comforting warmth. She looks up to the Liguna, who grabs two of the rags by the bowl of water. Handing one to Alice, Danahlia wipes away her own tears and the snot running from her nose, giving Alice a smirk. Alice grins back, doing the same. The fox wants to say something, apologize or give thanks, but when her mouth opens she can't seem to find the words. The girls just look at each other for a moment before

Danahlia turns and crawls over to one of the bed rolls. Alice settles on her own. They exchange goodnights before quickly falling asleep.

Chapter 5

Carton

They can't tell what time it is in the cellar but it seems terribly early when Ms. Ringtail wakes them. Twinkaleni must have given her the mushrooms the girls had gathered in the swamp because the soup she brings has plenty of them. The motherly Lotarin joins them for breakfast and encouraged the girls to eat quickly so they can start on their chores before it gets too hot out. During the morning meal, the raccoon woman reveals she had always wanted children but the war had taken her husband before they could have any, and so is especially happy to have her three young guests.

After, Ms. Ringtail has Alice and Twinkaleni do a little light gardening for her, which consists mostly of pulling a few pesky weeds. She takes pride in telling them of the "secret" techniques she employs to determine a vegetable's readiness to be picked or pulled up from the ground. She also demonstrates by harvesting several crops for their dinner.

Before the sun can reach its strongest, the girls are taken back inside where Danahlia has been cleaning. They have a break and are then freed to do as they please. Danahlia must stay indoors to ensure a low profile but Twinkaleni and Alice decide to explore the town. Ms. Ringtail gives them a small cask to fill at the well and the girls head out.

Carton turns out to be quite lively despite its size. Shops and stalls replace houses as they near the center and people hustle about their business as shopkeepers call enticing praises for their wares. Alice zigzags along the street, unable to help looking at all there is at offer. Fancy fabrics and fully made garments, pots and other earthen wares, fruits and vegetables, cooked and raw meats, and freshly baked goods line the streets. She even sees some live chickens in tiny cages. She squats before the cages, watching the imprisoned birds jerking their heads around as if trying to watch everything around them at once while clucking nervously.

Twinkaleni has to back track to find her. When she does, the little Murin taps her shoulder, "Alice, I believe I have found someone who may be interested in our remaining core stones."

The Murin leads her to a stall consisting of several tables, all with elaborate bits of jewelry. A young, dark furred Feladine girl, perhaps of an age with Twinkaleni, though a bit taller, shouts to the passer-byes while gesturing grandly at the tables, "Best necklaces, rings, and bracelets in all of Arsalia!

Jewels and gems from far and wide! Only the best, for the best, all right here!"

The stall's owner, presumably the younger cat girl's mother, is occupied by other patrons. The two browse the tables' glittering wares as they wait, Twinkaleni standing on her tippy-toes to see.

Alice had never worn jewelry but her mother had had several pieces. She recognizes rings and necklaces easily enough, but she wonders how some of the others would be worn. Some pieces consist of pearl white cloth with jewels and gold filigree sewn right into the fabric. She thinks they might look nice wrapped around the arm or even tail. Other pieces look as if they might go over one's ear.

"Ffft ffft!" Hisses the younger Feladine, waving Alice and Twinkaleni away, "Customers only, no gawkers."

"We *are* customers. We're waitin' to talk to her," counters Alice, pointing to the cat woman.

The younger Feladine looks to the older then back to Alice, yellow feline eyes narrowing, "My mom's busy and you don't look like you have any money," the girl then crosses her arms, "And if you don't have money, you don't have business, and if you don't have business, you don't have no business bein' here," she claims in a way that sounds rehearsed.

"But we do. We seek to trade," assures Twinkaleni, turning her back to Alice.

Alice sets down the empty cask to rummage inside Twinkaleni's backpack to pull out a few core stones, showing them to the girl, "We have these. We'd like to sell 'em."

The cat girl looks closely at the glowing core stones, her eyes widening. "Oh," she murmurs in awe and tries to pick one up only to have Alice close her fingers around them.

"Do *you* have any money?" Alice asks, pulling them away.

The Feladine narrows her eyes again and then makes her way to her mother. She tugs on the woman's dress, speaking up to her while pointing at Alice and Twinkaleni. The shop owner looks away from her conversation to her daughter and then glances at the two waiting girls. With a negligent shake of her head and a few words, she returns to her other potential customers. The cat girl persists and is eventually given a small purse. She returns to Alice and Twinkaleni, examining the contents without revealing it.

The young Feladine then tucks the purse away into a pocket on her beige dress, "So, how much you want for those glowin' gems?"

Alice had little experience with actual money. She looks to Twinkaleni, who shrugs, and then back at the girl, "How much you got?"

"Why don't you tell me how much you want and we'll go from there?" the girl says, stepping closer to Alice, standing as tall as she can.

"Why don't *you* tell me how much you got and then we can discuss how much *I* want?" says Alice, matching the smaller girl's posture.

The Feladine doesn't back down, instead saying louder, "Why don't *you* tell me how much you want 'em for, and *I'll* tell you how many I want?"

Not wanting to lose any position in the bargaining, Alice practically shouts, "Well why don't *you* tell me how much you got and *I'll* tell *you* how many you can have?!"

The two escalate, throwing their conditions at each other until their noses are practically touching while Twinkaleni looks uncertainly between them. The other customers leave without purchase and the mother turns to the arguing pair, hissing, "Katia! Why are you yelling?!"

The irritation in the cat woman's tone startles Alice and the cat girl into silence, their ears folding back as she approaches angrily, hands moving to her hips as she waits for a response.

Katia whines, "These girls have core stones and won't tell me how much they want for 'em even though I asked over and over."

The mother looks to Alice in surprise, "Core stones? Let me see them, child."

Alice reveals the ones in her hand and the mother looks at them much like her daughter first had, "Mm, how many do you have and what colors?"

Alice looks to Twinkaleni, who then lists off their inventory, "Six red, three blue, four brown, and eight green."

"I'll take the lot. What do you say to... ten glints?" the mother offers.

Alice looks to Twinkaleni, who takes her by the hand, saying to the Feladine mother, "Allow me to confer with my colleague for a moment."

The two take several steps away, then Twinkaleni tugs on Alice's hand getting her to bend over and offer an ear.

The Murin whispers, "What is the worth of a glint?"

Alice whispers back, "I don't know, I never handled much money."

Twinkaleni takes a glance back at the waiting Feladine before whispering again, "They seem quite interested in acquiring our core stones, perhaps it is a fair bargain."

In Alice's experience trading, the first offer was never the best and she whispers back, "Let me handle this."

She turns back and approaches the Feladine, "We'll need at least fifteen glints. These are rare stones after all."

"Ha!" scoffs Katia, but before she can say anymore, her mother puts her tail in front of her daughter's mouth.

The mother then counters, "Only the red and blue are worth noting, the rest I can take or leave, eleven glints."

"They're all of good size. We can't take less than fourteen for 'em," Alice tosses back as if already disinterested.

"Twelve, for all," counters the mother, her tail twitching.

"Thirteen," Alice demands.

The mother Feladine takes in a long breath and then says, "Show them all to me then. I want to see each one."

Twinkaleni and Alice pull out their stock of cores, holding them out for inspection. The mother Feladine takes one up and shoos her daughter away when she tries to do the same. The cat woman looks at several of the cores, rolling them around to see them from different angles and holding them under the shade of her hand to examine their glows. Alice begins to feel a bit anxious, standing there like some criminal awaiting sentence.

After several long minutes, the woman smiles, "Deal, thirteen glints for the lot. Let me just get my purse."

Alice lets out a relieved breath and Twinkaleni beams up at her. Katia retrieves a small wooden box and opens it to Alice saying, "Alright, alright, put 'em in here. And I'm counting." The box contains several unset gems and precious stones. The girls place their cores into the box and Katia snaps it shut when they finish.

Alice asks, "Your mom makes all this jewelry?"

"Best in all Arsalia," claims Katia as her mother returns.

The Feladine woman drops thirteen gold coins into Alice's hand, counting each one out. Doing everything she can to hide her excitement, Alice graciously thanks the woman, hoists up the empty cask, and wanders off into the street, her tail wagging wildly.

"Well done, Alice!" Twinkaleni exclaims, hopping excitedly along at her side.

Alice grins, handing the little mage a coin, "Look, they're so beautiful."

Alice had never handled gold before but looking at the coins now, she can see why it would be so valued. The surface of each small disc glitters with the afternoon sun in a most mesmerizing way. She angles a coin to catch the light and finds they're all stamped with a regal lion's head and minuscule bits of writing along the edges.

"Is that the king?" Alice asks, tapping at the tiny image.

"Mmm, according to the inscription, that would be King Ghadhanfar the second, Ghadhanfar the third, who's death ignited the current Blood War, must have been his son. That must mean that these coins where minted sometime before King Ghadhanfar the third's coronation. He really didn't rule for very long at all."

"What happened to 'im?" Alice asks, rubbing her thumb over a coin's surface.

"That is a great mystery. King Ghadhanfar the second was already quite old when his only son was born. Once Ghadhanfar the thirds father had passed, he was named king, as is custom. Only a few years into his reign, the still young Ghadhanfar the third died rather suddenly. With no heir of his own, Arsalia is now kingless and run primarily by the Royal Council."

Walking down the street, Alice wonders, "How do you know all this stuff?"

Twinkaleni grins, "I speculate on some details, but such things have happened in the past. This entire war could even just be a cat's-paw for someone intending to take the throne for themselves."

"A cat's-paw?" Alice asks, thinking of the Feladine they just dealt with.

Twinkaleni explains a theory she had cobbled together from what the mages were told and what she has read of politics and the history of Arsalia back when she was studying under the Order of Thermathrogi.

Frequently, when a king would perish with no heir, a struggle of some sort would ensue as various factions attempted to seize power. Often the struggle would be internal and possibly lead to a civil war, though it is not unheard of for the factions to direct their hostility toward a common enemy, such as in the Blood War. Twinkaleni is sure to note that this is the forth Blood War and that such a conflict would weaken some political factions while strengthening others.

Alice wonders how anyone could benefit from a war and Twinkaleni goes on to say, "Suppose during this war, your lands are far from the conflict and remain safe, allowing you to field large armies that claim several key victories over the enemy. This would not only put you in a stronger position over your rivals, who have had battles on their own lands and thus have had their strength diminished and their populaces suffer, but victories would grant you glory and the support of the people."

As they search for the town well, the Murin mage goes on in length, revealing various instances she has read about. It seems strange to Alice that people would take advantage of their own in such ways but can imagine how desirable ruling an entire country might be. As the little mouse prattles on, she imagines herself as a queen. Rich and powerful, she sits on a massive golden throne within a great hall with servants to attend to her every need. She wonders what a queen does with all her time, sitting around with no concerns seems like it would get boring. Then she imagines herself as a warrior queen, Jellybane in hand, the head of armies, facing down legions of monsters, and bringing peace to the world. The image makes her grin.

The girls find the well near the center of town and fill the cask before heading back to Ms. Ringtail's house. It's late in the evening when they arrive and Alice's arms are terribly sore from carrying the heavy water. She's relieved when the raccoon woman meets them in the front yard to take it from her.

"Thank you, dears. I know luggin' this around can be quite a chore," she admits, taking the cask inside, the girls following. "So, how was your stroll 'round town? Find what you were lookin' for?"

"Oh yes, Alice did quite well in negotiating prices for our core stones," says Twinkaleni, smiling up at the Tokala.

Alice proudly holds out the gold coins to show Ms. Ringtail, "We got thirteen glints for 'em."

"Thirteen glints?" Ms. Ringtail exclaims, looking back to the girls and nearly losing her hold on the cask as she sets it down in the kitchen. "Goodness, I had no idea they were worth so much.

Oh, don't go showin' 'em off like that, girl. You never know who might be watchin'."

Alice closes her fingers over the coins as Ms. Ringtail hurries into another room. She returns with a small cloth purse.

"Put 'em in here for safe keepin'," she says, handing it to Alice. Alice does and they jingle satisfactorily as she places the purse into her trouser pocket. Ms. Ringtail nods, "Good. Now pull 'em out only when you need 'em. Times are tough and thieves might be lurkin' anywhere."

Twinkleni holds out the coin she was carrying to the woman, "For your trouble, please take it."

Ms. Ringtail smiles broadly, accepts the coin, and strokes the mouse girl's cheek, "You girls are no trouble at all, thank you. Your friend is in the cellar. Why don't you go see her? Supper's nearly done, I'll bring it down in a minute."

The girls thank Ms. Ringtail for her kindness and head down to see Danahlia. They find her napping on one of the bed rolls and gently wake her.

"Huh? Oh, hey guys. How was town?" she asks groggily, sitting up.

Twinkaleni answers, "Alice has gotten us a fair sum of money for our core stones. I believe we may have enough to replace all that we lost in the Muck."

Alice grins and pulls a few coins from the purse to show, their golden surfaces glittering beautifully even in the faint candle light.

"Wags! How many did you get?" Danahlia asks, holding out her hand.

Alice gives her a few coins, "We have twelve now."

"Twelve glints! We should be able to get plenty o' stuff. That means we can get outta here. I mean, Ms. Ringtail's been great, but I'm not a fan of staying cooped up indoors like this."

"Yes, we really shouldn't impose any more than we must," adds Twinkaleni.

Alice purses her lips, "Yeah, I guess."

This was the first settlement outside of Toki she had ever been to and wouldn't have minded if they could look around a bit more before leaving. Though she understands her companions' desire to do so. As far as they knew, they were still being hunted after all.

"You girls aren't talkin' 'bout leavin' already are you?" asks, Ms. Ringtail, entering the chamber with another steaming bowl of soup. The trio makes way for her so she can place it on the table.

"Not immediately, we still have to replace what we lost getting here," assures Twinkaleni.

"Yeah, and with the money Alice got, we should be able to get plenty more," adds Danahlia, making Alice smile.

"Well, that's good to hear. Where're you all headin'?" Ms. Ringtail asks, handing out spoons.

They hadn't really made plans on a specific destination and so Ms. Ringtail tells them of some possible stops they may want to make in nearby towns and villages. They all eat together, discussing preparations for their eventual departure. Ms. Ringtail proves to be very knowledgeable of various local shops they should visit to gather their needed supplies. The girls are yawning when their host wishes them goodnight and they go to sleep.

The next morning, after a few chores, Alice and Twinkaleni head off in search of supplies. Their first stop is at a stall that sells various bags and pouches. They buy two large backpacks for one of their glints to replace the ones they had lost to the awful culicades and the giant toads of, what Ms. Ringtail refers to as, the Southern Muck. They then move on to purchase various other items, a small iron pot, extra clothes, food, and even a map.

Glints are worth quite a lot and many of the items they purchase are not worth a whole glint alone. This has the girls ending up with a few shils, silver coins, and many brins, bronze coins. They also become acquainted with the monetary value of each as they shop. Twelve brins is equal to one shil, while six shils adds up to one glint.

As Alice is finishing a purchase of some dried salted meat, Danahlia having made several mentions of the need to acquire some the night before and then again this morning, Twinkaleni appears from down the street and practically drags her to an elderly Houdain sitting on the ground. The canine man's legs are crossed, with a sheet of burgundy cloth under and before him. Atop the cloth are several books. As they approach, the old man looks to Twinkaleni and smiles wearily, his face and ears drooping with age. His coat may have been brown once, patches still lightly colored so, but now he was so far past graying that the fur around his mouth is turning white.

"This man has a most remarkable volume in stock, a combination bestiary and herbiary!" exclaims Twinkaleni, pointing to a particularly thick tome.

Alice had only seen a few books in her life and this one had to be the biggest by far.

"What's that?" she asks, peering at its plain forest green cover.

"May I?" Twinkaleni asks the old man. He nods, a subtle movement, still smiling.

Twinkaleni hefts the book in her small hands, opening it to show Alice a page with a highly detailed drawing of some sort of plant. There are notes beside the plant and lines from the notes to different parts of it, the flowers, the leaves, the stem, and the roots.

"This book has detailed information on various plants, ferals, and monsters, we may encounter. It can tell us what is edible and what isn't, what dangers to look and prepare for, and even about creatures we can hunt and how best to go about it!" the little mouse bubbles, clearly very excited about her discovery.

She opens the book to another section and reveals a drawing of some sort of unpleasant looking creature that walks on two squat legs, has little to no fur, lanky arms, and a large angular nose.

Alice points to it, "Ew, what is that?"

"It says it's a boggart, a creature that inhabits swamps and other wetlands. And look at this," Twinkaleni says, quickly flipping through several pages to stop at one that has a drawing that resembles the amphibian creatures from the Muck.

Alice points to it, "Hey, that looks like the giant toads that were eating those huge mosquitoes."

"Indeed. They are known as Greater Anuragoata. As we already know, their legs are edible, but according to this book, much of the rest of them are too. It goes on to say that they are commonly hunted for their meat and skins which have a variety of applications."

"Wags. So you want this book? How much is it?"

The elderly Houdain holds up four boney fingers as Twinkaleni answers, "He would like four glints for it."

"Four?!" Alice blurts, shocked any one thing could cost so much, "That's almost all our money, and didn't *you* say we should try to save some for later?"

Twinkaleni closes the large book and holds it to her chest protectively, "I know, I know, but I believe the knowledge this will grant us will be well worth it."

Alice looks to the cute little mouse girl, her massive ears folded back, amber eyes (somehow larger than usual) pleading, tiny pink nose quivering, and whiskers twitching. Alice sighs and digs around in her purse to gather up the last of their glints. As she drops them in the old man's outstretched hand, the Murin mage practically leaps with joy, making adorable little noises while hugging her new book. The old man says nothing, only nodding a few times at what Alice hopes is a bargain well struck.

Fully stocked, the girls make their way back to Ms. Ringtail's. Alice has to keep watch over Twinkaleni as they walk, as the mage's eyes never leave the pages of her book and several times she has to guide the little mouse girl back from wandering off or nearly running into people and walls. The only time the Murin's head pops up is when a delicious warm scent catches her attention.

Her nose sniffs at the air, leading her and Alice to a small bakery. A little Lagomorph boy is busily arranging delectable looking pastries of some sort. At the girls' approach, his long rabbit ears perk up a second before he turns to them. He smiles brightly, moving away so they can browse his wares.

Twinkaleni follows her nose to some pastries that look to be stuffed to bursting with cheese. Others are topped with fruits, nuts, or honey, and all look terribly tempting. Twinkaleni is entranced by the ones oozing cheddar and Alice decides to buy her one. She then uses what little remains of their money to buy an assorted set of the cakes to bring back to Ms. Ringtail and Danahlia. The girls find it difficult not to tear into the small stack of baked goods but manage to get them all safely to the house. Once there, they add a few of their purchases and the pastries to the evening meal, having a feast to mark their last night with the generous Lotarin.

As everyone is enjoying dinner, Danahlia reaches for Twinkaleni's book, asking, "Where'd you get that?"

The Murin beats back the lizard girl's hand with a spoon, squeaking, "No, Danny, you'll smudge the pages!" She then points the spoon at the larger girl's pastry sticky fingers.

Alice grins, "We bought it from some old guy. Cost four whole glints."

"Four glints?!" Danahlia blurts, crumbs flying free from her mouth. "We could've eaten over a month on that!" she whines, reaching for the tome again.

Twinkaleni pulls the book off the table and out of reach, "Money well spent, I assure you."

"I'm sure it was," adds Ms. Ringtail, "That looks like one of Mr. Bernard's works. Word is, he was quite the adventurer in his day, traveled all over the world explorin' every inch of Arsalia and beyond. I'm quite surprised he let it go for only four glints."

"Only?" exclaims Danahlia.

"The knowledge in this book will be invaluable to us, Danny. That money could have kept us fed for a month or more, but this book will teach us how to feed ourselves for a life time," claims Twinkaleni, tapping the book with a tiny finger.

Danahlia eyes the book, unimpressed, "How? We gonna eat it?"

"Don't be silly. Look here."

Everyone leans in to look at the pages Twinkaleni opens the book to. It has several detailed drawings of a mushroom from different angles with writing linked to various bits, including the cap, gills, and stem. Alice recognizes the mushroom from one they saw back at the shack they stayed in during the recent heavy rain.

She points this out and Twinkaleni nods, "Indeed, but we didn't dare eat it because we didn't know if it was poisonous or not. This book says it is edible, not only that but it goes on to say where more can be found and what seasons are best to harvest them. With this to guide our efforts, we can practically live off the land."

"Which means we won't need to risk goin' into as many towns," Alice adds.

Danahlia makes an approving sound and reaches for the book again, only to get another sharp rap on her fingers from Twinkaleni's spoon.

After dinner, the girl's had planned to slip out once darkness set in, but Ms. Ringtail convinces them to stay for one more night so they can resume their journey well rested in the early morning. When the time comes, the trio is eager to be on their way. Ms. Ringtail had spent the night stitching up a few bits of their clothing, being sure to at least finish Danahlia's cloak. The kind woman, gives them a few more bandages, though there wounds have all but healed, and a few hand fulls of her precious vegetables for the road. They thank her again and she gives them each a hug.

"Oh, every time," she fusses, getting teary eyed, "You girls take care of each other, you hear?"

They whisper their goodbyes and depart under the cover of the yet sunless morning.

Chapter 6

Forest Children

The girls head roughly north from Carton, intent on making their way through a forest to help hide their trail. They walk together, Danahlia holding the map at different angles while Twinkaleni points out entries of interest from her book, reading aloud the descriptions of plants, animals, and monsters. Whenever an interesting plant catches her eye, Alice asks if it's mentioned in the book. Many are, and the trio's confidence in their ability to live off the land is bolstered every time they manage to identify something edible. Alice picks many of these edible plants and flowers so the girls can sample them. Though most are not particularly appetizing, they find it fun to try the abundant local flora. As they walk, the landscape steadily becomes woodier, the distance they can see dwindling as trees replace fields and the sun begins to descend.

Under an orange tinted sky, the girls settle down for the night. With their supply of ready-to-eat foods, there is no need for a fire so they sit together, eating and drinking from their stores. Despite the day long walk, Twinkaleni is still reading from her book until the last rays of light finally get her to stop. They make beds of the thick lush grass and pillows of their packs. The late summer air is still plenty warm, letting sleep claim the tired adventures quickly.

In the night, something disturbs Alice's rest. A faint noise, quiet but nearby, it sounds like voices. She groans, her eyes heavy and body sluggish, as she forces herself to move. It should be pitch black at this hour she knows but is surprised to find that she can see. Subtle green light is just visible through the long grasses around her. Alice struggles to push herself up on her elbows to peer over it and finds the light is coming from a green core stone. It's sitting on Danahlia's chest, while Twinkaleni cradles the larger girl's head in her lap, the Murin saying something in a soothing whisper that's too faint for Alice to make out.

She tries to speak but only mumbles, alerting the other two. She tries again groggily asking, "What's, what's goin' on?"

Danahlia sniffs wetly, "Nothing, just, just go back to sleep, ok?" Her voice is uncharacteristically subdued.

Alice is about to inquire further but Twinkaleni adds, "It's alright, Alice. Everything is just fine."

"You still have a core?" Alice asks, looking at the uncommonly bright sphere.

"Yes, the one I enchanted. Now go back to sleep, we have another long walk ahead," the mouse mage says.

Vision and mind still blurry from sleep, Alice settles back down and drifts off once more.

The following morning's breakfast is a strangely silent affair. Alice is curious about the goings on of last night but isn't sure she should ask. When they begin walking again, the trio carries on as they usually do, Danahlia singing a little tune to herself about traveling a few steps ahead of the other two. Twinkaleni keeps pace with Alice while looking at her book, though less talkative than usual. Alice, prone to curiosity, wrestles with how best to inquire about what she saw.

She is about to try to broach the subject, when Twinkaleni whisper, "She still has nightmares."

"What?" Alice whispers back.

Twinkaleni looks up from her book to the Liguna, replying, "About the night her family was taken from her, among other things."

"Oh," Alice says glumly.

She watches Danahlia, striding confidently forward through the thickening trees as if without a single care in the entire world. She recalls from the night before, that wet sniff. Had she been crying? The young Tokala looks around the woods, trying to think of something to say. Something calming or caring, something to let Danahlia know that she was there too and could offer some comfort as Twinkaleni had. She is considering this when a weight shifts slightly on her back.

Reaching casually to adjust her sword, Alice yips when she feels the burning sting of a cut. Jerking her hand away, she finds thin slices on her palm and several fingers, blood only just beginning to drip from them. Twinkaleni and Danahlia abruptly turn to her.

Twinkaleni peers at her injured hand, "Alice, what happened?"

While Danahlia shouts, "Hey! Give that back!"

Alice follows the angry Liguna's gaze up over her head to find her sword in the hands of a grinning Lobovan. The wolf girl is dangling upside down from a tree branch a few feet above her head. With impressive agility, the girl swings herself back up to stand on the branch, holding Jellybane before her admiringly, "Now this is nice."

"Give back my sword!" Alice growls, baring her teeth.

The wolf girl looks down at them, her coat of sandy tones, tans, browns, and some grays, wearing little more than rags for a shirt and pants. She tilts her head to one side, "Yours? It rather looks like it's mine now, Red."

"Give it back, or I'm gonna shove my spear so far up your furry little butt, you'll taste it!" Danahlia snarls, taking a two handed grip on her weapon.

"Oh, you think my butt's little?" the Lobovan sneers, shaking her rump while wagging her thick full tail tauntingly down at them.

"That's it. Twinkie, blast 'er!" Danahlia orders.

"Uh, Danny," the mouse mage says warily, glancing around. Her tone of voice alerts Alice and she looks to find a group of plant-like monsters appearing silently from behind trees and bushes all around them. There are nearly a dozen of them and worse, they're armed.

The creatures vary in size from Danahlia's height to one being even smaller than Twinkaleni. All look menacing with their wooden spears and strangely distorted faces, lacking in any symmetry. They appear to have been summoned up from the surrounding forest, their coloring and features blend so well with the thick foliage. Alice recalls Twinkaleni mentioning some time ago that magic could allow some people to create their own servants and soldiers. The wolf girl didn't look like much, but then, neither did Twinkaleni.

"Danny," Alice calls nervously.

With complete focus still on the wolf girl, Danahlia growls, "Fine."

Shoving her spear into Alice's hands she tosses off her cloak and immediately begins scaling the tree with anger fueled haste. Her clawed hands and taloned feet gouge bark from the large oak as she races to meet the thieving Lobovan on her branch. Despite her injury, Alice grips the spear in both hands and waves it at the ring of silent monsters. Some shift restlessly as if waiting for an opening to attack, while others watch the lizard girl climb.

Twinkaleni shifts to Alice's back, holding her large book tightly to her chest.

Perhaps surprised at Danahlia's speed or that she had revealed herself to be a Liguna, the wolf girl hesitates until Danahlia is nearly upon her. She swings the sword at the climbing girl but clearly has no practice with such weapons. Danahlia easily ducks the blow, the blade biting and lodging into the thick tree's trunk. The lizard girl then uses her long tail to whip at the other girl's ankles. The Lobovan, trying to free the sword, loses her balance and falls gracelessly to the ground before Alice.

Alice puts the point of the spear to the stunned wolf's throat and demands she call off her monsters. Danahlia, having freed Alice's sword, leaps down to join them, noticing the ring of creatures for the first time.

"Twinkie, what are these things?" she asks cautiously, raising Jellybane to them.

Twinkaleni starts to rapidly flip through her book, "I, I'm not sure, some kind of plant golems perhaps."

The downed wolf girl groans, "Ugh, they're wild monsters. Very territorial," she grins then, "And guess where you're standin'."

Danahlia kneels down to roughly grab one of the Lobovan's ears, placing the sword's edge to her throat, "Call 'em off or I swear, I'll get you before they get us."

"No! Don't hurt Lyca!" cries a little voice. The girls turn to see the smallest of the monsters running towards them. Its face falls off to reveal it's only a mask made from mosses, mud, and leaves disguising a teary eyed Murin boy.

One of the larger creatures tries to grab him but misses, and the boy falls over the wolf girl protectively, sniffling.

"Nezu," the Lobovan groans disapprovingly, taking the boy under an arm.

"What the tick is this?" Danahlia growls angrily.

Alice looks more closely at the ring of now nervously shifting creatures and begins to see some irregularities. An ear or nose poking out here and there from under masks and a few tails dangling behind legs give the creatures away.

"They're kids," she says in surprise.

The tall one that tried to take hold of the mouse boy removes a bit of moss from a long equine face revealing himself to be an Echanian. He drops his spear and takes a step forward.

"Please, don't hurt them. We never meant to harm anyone," he says in the quavering voice of a boy on the cusp of manhood.

"Could've fooled me. She almost took my head off," Danahlia grumbles, lowering Jellybane.

"Psh, you came out of it ok," tosses back the wolf girl, Lyca, with a sneer.

Danahlia raises the sword again, but Twinkaleni grabs her by the arm, "I think that is enough foolishness for one day."

Danahlia lets out a breath through her nostrils, stands up, and trades weapons with Alice. Lyca stares at them for a moment before getting to her knees and checking on the crying Murin boy. Nezu appears to be even younger than Twinkaleni, though is only slightly smaller. Alice looks to the Echanian, who's getting the small band to reveal themselves. He is lean, strong, and though mud and leaves cover most of him, she can see his coat is a deep chestnut brown with an ebony mane.

"Who are you all? And why'd you attack us?" she demands of him.

He looks to her with tired hazel eyes but Lyca answers, "We weren't *attackin'* you. We just thought we'd... lighten your load a bit."

"You're common thieves then," Twinkaleni remarks distastefully.

"We're not thieves!" Lyca growls, and then haughtily adds, "We haven't stolen anything yet."

"You tried. That just makes you *bad* thieves," says Danahlia, looking down at the wolf girl.

The Lobovan bristles, jumping to her feet to match Danahlia's stare, despite being a bit shorter and unarmed. The tiny Murin boy is grasping her hand and she's about to say something when the Echanian calls loudly, "We're sorry for the trouble. We're just trying to get some food."

"Shut up, Philip," Lyca orders, still locking gazes with Danahlia.

"Maybe they can help us."

"I said, shut up!" Lyca roars, baring her canine teeth at him.

"You try stealin' from us, and then ask for help? You got some nerve," Alice growls, checking her cut hand. The cuts across her palm and several fingers bleed and burn, but are very thin and, she guesses, not deep.

"I'm sorry. We didn't have a choice," explains Philip, "So many of us are sick and the forest has become too dangerous. We need food and medicine but we can't afford either."

"Sick?" Twinkaleni asks, "What from?"

Tensions slowly settle as the horse boy tells them of a sort of plant that has been spreading in the forest, and now even more so after the recent rain. From what he says, once the plant matures it produces bubbles that float about until they hit something. The moment anything solid touches their delicate skin, the bubbles pop, releasing a powder that makes you sick. He goes on to say that this plant has forced them from their usual hunting and gathering grounds.

"How many of you are there?" Alice asks, licking her hand before Danahlia helps her wrap it in on of Ms. Ringtail's bandages.

"They don't need to know that," Lyca is quick to say.

Philip answers anyway, "Almost two dozen, though half of us are sick now."

Of the handful of forest dwellers, Lyca and Philip seem to be the oldest. The others are of various species but all look ragged, thin, and nervous.

Lyca glares at Philip as he talks and stomps over to him, saying in obvious irritation, "Philip, a word."

She then grabs the tall boy's wrist and yanks him a few feet away to whisper angrily, the tiny Murin, Nesu, never leaving her side. The others watch Alice's party and their two companions uncertainly. Alice, Danahlia, and Twinkaleni gather to confer with each other.

"What should we do?" asks Alice.

Danahlia jerks her head to the side, "Let's get outta here, we don't owe 'em nothin'."

Twinkaleni rubs one of her ears between two fingers, "This plant and the sickness it brings concerns me. It might be best to avoid the forest all together. They themselves may already be afflicted."

Alice shakes her head, "I don't think we can walk all the way around this forest. Did you guys see how big it was on the map?"

"Yeah, we can't go around, but I don't like the idea of us walkin' around here with *these* guys," says Danahlia, eyeing the strangers, "They already tried to rob us once."

"I think they only did it because they're desperate," suggests Alice.

"Perhaps," nods Twinkaleni, "They say many of them are sick, which would mean they need food not only for themselves but their companions as well, though this is assuming they're telling the truth about this sickness and their numbers."

"Look at 'em," says Alice, "One thing I'm sure their tellin' the truth about is that they need food."

The girls glance over at the handful of muddy kids. With their masks off, Alice can see the gauntness of their cheeks, the uncertainty in their eyes, and the grim frowns on their faces. She had seen the same plenty of times in Toki village when there just wasn't enough food or room to go around. Many children who had lost their parents had to sleep outside with nothing but the grumbling of their stomachs to comfort them. She herself had been there often enough before she learned to support herself.

Danahlia looks sharply away from them and grumbles, "What're we supposed to do about it?"

"We should help," encourages Alice, "I don't think they're lyin'."

"How do you propose we do that?" inquires Twinkaleni.

"Well, we're pretty well stocked on food. And like you said, we can use that to find more," Alice assures, pointing to Twinkaleni's book.

"Whoa, whoa, you are not seriously sayin' we should give 'em all our food are you?!" Danahlia exclaims.

Alice shakes her head, "Not all of it. Just some, just so they can get by."

"But they said there's like twenty of 'em. And what about that bubble-makin'-gettin'-people-sick plant they were talkin' about?" Danahlia argues.

"Perhaps we can aid in that as well. We will need more information first, but if there is an entry in this guide, it may tell us something of value about treating this illness," says Twinkaleni, holding up her book.

"Oh come on, not you too. We have enough trouble takin' care of ourselves. We can't feed all these guys, we don't even know 'em," Danahlia points out.

"Many times in the past we were in need of help, Danny, and the only reason we've survived this long is because perfect strangers offered us what little they had," Twinkaleni reminds, "Now it is our turn. We might be these people's only chance."

Alice nods, "We have to at least try. It's the right thing to do, you know it is."

Danahlia shakes her head in defeat, "Fine."

In agreement, the girls set down their packs and begin removing bits of food. Alice offers out a loaf of hard baked bread to the weary strangers, who look at her and the others in confusion. Twinkaleni and Danahlia follow suit, holding out some cheese and Danahlia even offers some of her precious dried meat.

The dirty children are hesitant to accept and Danahlia shakes her offering, grumbling, "Go on, take it."

A glimmer of hope enters their weary eyes and a few step forward only to have Lyca shout, "Hey! What's this?"

The wolf girl stomps over to the trio, Alice telling her, "It's what we can spare."

Lyca looks to her with some mix of wariness, anger, and perhaps something else.

Joining her, Philip asks, "You're, giving this to us? Even after we tried to rob you?"

"Yeah, you guys aren't gonna make it as thieves," snickers Danahlia.

Lyca growls, "We don't need-"

But as she raises her hand to slap at Alice's offering, Philip catches her wrist, "Don't be stubborn, Lyca. We *do* need their help."

The Lobovan glares at the Echanian, her lips rising over sharp teeth, but then her stomach burbles audibly. She huffs and turns away. Philip slowly accepts Alice's bread, and then grins widely once he has it. The horse boy immediately begins to break it into pieces, offering them to the other children. A few others accept the girls' offerings gratefully, smiles slow to reach their cheeks as if they hadn't done it in a while. The girls hand out a good chunk of their supplies, but feel warm satisfaction in doing so.

Philip thanks the girls profusely and they get a little better acquainted. Then, as a group, they all head deeper into the forest. As they walk, he explains that Lyca and he were from the same town. The wolf girl had lost her parents, much as Alice had, and he was sent away by his mother in the hopes that he would avoid being drafted into the war that had already claimed his father.

The two left together and drifted for a while, occasionally finding other orphans and those with nowhere else to go wandering or near villages. Once their numbers had swollen to the point that traveling would be dangerous, they decided to settle in the forest. Life here had never been easy for them but they survived on what they could hunt and gather. That was until the recent heavy rain brought about a rapid growth to the horrible plants.

Philip recounts that they grew deep in the forest and seemed harmless, but once it started to rain, they began producing the illness inducing bubbles that would detach from the main plant and float off. Twinkaleni is particularly curious about this plant and flips through her book, asking questions.

She eventually points out an entry and asks, "Is this the plant?"

Philip, much taller than the Murin mage, leans over her shoulder to see, "Yeah, I think that looks like them."

"Excellent. According to this book, those aren't plants at all but a type of fungi called, the floating puffball."

Danahlia snorts, "That's a funny name."

"Indeed," Twinkaleni continues, "it says here that the floating bubbles you refer to are its sporangium. They contain its spores, or seeds. It also confirms what you say about the sickness."

"Does it say anything about a cure?" asks Alice.

"Uh, yes, here, it says the young fungus can be harvested and brewed with water into a tea that should help dissipate the symptoms. But, only the younger fungi that have not yet formed a sporangium are suitable."

Philip's eyes widen and he places a hopeful hand on Twinkaleni's tiny shoulder, "Does that mean you can heal our friends?"

"Uh, um, well, potentially, given that we can, acquire the necessary immature fungi," she stammers.

"That's great! You hear that? We can make a cure!" announces Philip, raising a fist to his companions. They join him in a little cheer and even Lyca seems pleased with the news.

Curious, Alice walks beside the wolf girl and asks, "You guys don't seem all that surprised that Danny is a Liguna."

Lyca looks to her with a sneer, "Pff, she's not so special. We had two Cold Bloods with us a little while ago but they didn't wanna stick around."

Danahlia takes great interest in this and begins asking about her kin. Amused, Lyca reveals they were a brother and sister pair who taught the others a bit about living off the land, what plants to eat, what to avoid, and even how to hunt. They left sometime before the floating puffballs began to be a problem. When asked about where they went, Lyca says they didn't say. Danahlia seems pleased to hear that more of her kind are around, but also a little disappointed she had missed them.

Alice wonders, "When was the last time you saw any of your people?"

"Me and Twinkie found one hiding out in a village a few months before we met," the lizard girl answers.

Lyca grins at Twinkaleni, "Twinkie? Ha! That's so cute."

"I know, right?" Danahlia smiles back.

Twinkaleni sighs.

Alice hears a few coughs coming from up ahead and the group picks up their pace. Soon they're among several more children, many of which are lying on the ground as a few others tend to them. Immediately, Lyca and Philip's group spread out to share what food was given to them, none of the small party eating a bite until then. They break for a short while to share a meal. The forest dwellers are ravenous, letting not a single crumb go to waste, but still giving each of their group equal shares. A small pool left by the rain gives the girls a chance to refill their water supply.

Philip almost immediately begins calling for volunteers to look for the fungus. Lyca, and by default Nesu, stand with him as a matter of course and a few others join them. Twinkaleni volunteers to go as well and, not wanting to leave her alone,

Danahlia and Alice decide to go too. A few of the volunteers take empty sacks with them and the group heads off to find the potentially lifesaving fungus.

The depths of the forest are dense and still damp, becoming more so the further they travel. Misty fog trapped under the thick canopy begins to limit their vision and they unconsciously huddle closer together. The knowledge Twinkaleni has gained from the book pays off as she is able to point out various edible plants. She double checks to be sure, and the party of nine plucks, picks, and unearths as they go, slowly refreshing their depleted food stores with various leaves, shoots, roots, and even a few mushrooms.

The group begins to disperse little by little, encouraged by their early success, prompting Lyca to warn them to stay together. As they search, Philip tells them they are heading in the general direction of their old camp site where they left much of their supplies, the floating puffballs having forced them to leave.

As he does, the little Murin boy, Nesu, tugs on the wolf girl's pant leg, pointing at a bush, "Lyca, saccha berries!"

The others become excited by the discovery and quickly approach only to have Lyca shout at them to stop. They obediently obey and Lyca tells them she had seen this particular bush before and that it had a floating puffball on it. She motions for Philip to investigate. Circling the berry bush, the horse boy points out that the puffball is still there. He waves for the new arrivals to come see so they know what to watch for.

Alice, Danahlia, and Twinkaleni circle to him cautiously and look to where he points. Nestled under a few of the bush's leaves and surrounded by bright pink berries, that have the clustered appearance of raspberries, is the puffball. It's a rather unpleasant looking, dirty flesh colored bubble the relative size of a fist with a few long hairs poking randomly out from it.

Twinkaleni looks closer, checking the book entry and Alice asks, "Can we move it?"

Philip shakes his head, "Nope, anything touches these things and they pop. It's rare that one would get caught like this without goin' off but I've seen it happen."

"And if this one detonates, its spores may contaminate the berries," adds Twinkaleni getting a nod from the Echanian.

"Can we get the berries on the other side?" asks Danahlia, referring to the other side of the bush.

"Don't risk it," warns Lyca, "A branch shifts too much and that thing can burst. We just have to leave it."

"Can you do anything about these things?" asks Alice, disappointed to be deterred by so small an obstacle.

Philip answers, "We used to throw rocks and sticks at 'em to get 'em to pop, but then a few days later the place would be covered with new growths."

"Have you tried burning them?" wonders Twinkaleni, peering at the puffball.

"Burnin' 'em?" asks Lyca, looking to Philip.

"Mm, no, we haven't done that. We haven't been able to get a fire going in a while with all this damp," he says, gesturing to the surrounding fog.

"Won't that just make 'em pop?" asks Alice.

Twinkaleni rubs one of her ears thoughtfully with a, "Mmm."

Danahlia looks to the little mage, "I know that look, whacha thinkin'?"

Instead of answering, Twinkaleni asks, "You've seen these puffballs floating around freely?"

"Um, yeah, I figure that's why they call 'em floatin' puffballs," says Lyca, Philip nodding.

After a few more moments of ear rubbing thought, Twinkaleni announces, "I wish to try something. Everyone step back."

Alice and Danahlia do, though the others look confused. Danahlia then uses the shaft of her spear to push a few back with her and Alice does the same with her arms, giving the Murin mage some room.

Lyca grumbles an irritated "Hey," but doesn't resist.

Once Twinkaleni is satisfied, she takes a few steps back herself, before pointing a finger to the puffball and shouting, "Feasta!"

Chapter 7

Puffball Tea

A thin, just barely visible thread of orange light zips toward the ugly bubble from the tip of Twinkaleni's finger. A loud pop accompanied by a whoosh of flame has everyone shouting out in surprise, ducking with eyes wide in search of danger.

Seeing no threat, Lyca demands, "What the tick was that?!" as she kneels to comfort a now crying Nesu.

Danahlia calls, "Twinkie?"

Surprised herself by the blast, Twinkaleni rolls from her bottom back to her feet, "My apologies everyone, but I believe it worked."

"What worked? What happened?" asks Alice, scanning the forest.

Philip points to the shaken berry bush, "The bubble, it's gone... and there's no powder."

"Indeed. As I suspected, the sporangium was filled with some kind of gas, which is how they are able to float. As it turns out, the gas is highly combustible. Upon contact with sufficient heat, the gas ignited, destroying the puffball and most, if not all, of the spores it contained."

Philip moves in to get a closer look at where the puffball was, "Does that mean it's safe?"

"I, I believe so, or at least, safer."

Philip touches some of the leaves, blackened by the blast.

"Any powder?" asks Lyca, taking a few steps closer, Nesu sniffling at her leg.

"Nope, none," the Echanian replies, "Looks like it's all gone," he then turns to Twinkaleni, "How'd you do that? You didn't have any fire."

"Oh, uh well, um..." Twinkaleni stammers.

"She can use magic," Danahlia announces proudly, giving the mouse mage a rough rub on the head as she passes to crouch by the berry bush.

The forest dwellers murmur among themselves, looking at the Murin mage curiously as Lyca laughs, "Magic? No way. Seriously, how'd you do that?"

"She *can* use magic," assures Alice, "I've seen her do it dozens o' times."

"Mmm, these are good," exclaims Danahlia, popping another berry into her mouth.

The others swiftly gather around, eager to get a share. As they pick and pluck the bush bare, Twinkaleni is bombarded with questions about her talent. None of the others had ever encountered anyone with such abilities before, the touch of magic being exceedingly rare in the world. Though she tries, the Murin mage's attempt to answer any one question is often interrupted by several more.

The bush isn't large but the group does get a few handfuls of berries before moving on. Eventually, Twinkaleni is tasked with feeling for each of the group's magical potential but has to inform them all that they had none. Disappointed but no less inquisitive, the group continues asking questions about magic, Alice and Danahlia pitching in answers where they can.

As they walk, the group finds several more puffballs, some floating, some still attached to their parent fungi. They make a game of being the first to point them out, eager to see Twinkaleni use her magic, and give a cheer for each one she destroys. Alice notices that even with some time between sightings, Twinkaleni's frequent use of her fire spell is starting to take its toll. The little mouse girl needs to take more deep breaths after each use and starts to slow in her pace. Lyca notices too and orders the group to begin avoiding the floating puffballs as they typically do.

Pressing on, the group encounters more and more of the hovering menaces. They often have to duck and weave past them, careful not to disturb their slow flight paths. The puffballs shift with the slightest breeze and everyone is grateful it isn't a windy day. Gathering food is significantly hampered as several members of the group need to keep watch while the others hurriedly take what they can. Fortunately, Philip is able to locate a young cluster of fungi that he says hasn't yet spawned any spores.

"See how dark it is? Their color begins to fade when they start makin' those floaters," the Echanian explains.

Alice looks over the fungal formation on a fallen tree. The splatter shape and uneven coloration make her think she could create something similar by throwing rotten tomatoes about.

"Is it safe to touch?" asks Danahlia, a clawed finger inches from it.

Philip nods, "Yeah, no one ever got sick from touching the dark patches, only after they were near a floater when it went off."

"How much do we need to make everyone better?" asks Lyca, using her nails to pull up some of the bark the fungus is growing on.

Twinkaleni consults her book, "I'm not sure, but we should probably collect as much as we can just to be safe."

"I can get it," says Alice, unsheathing her sword. The others step back and the fox girl places her sword against the downed tree to slowly and carefully remove as much of the fungus as possible. It has a sort of spongy texture that gives easily to Jellybane's razor edge, letting Alice take off much of it in one hunk.

"Good work, Red," Lyca comments, holding open a burlap sack reserved for the stuff.

Alice grins, placing the fungus into it. Cutting the fungus has produced a scent similar to damp soil but much stronger. Angling the sword, Alice manages to get a few more slices off the tree.

Once she places the rest in Lyca's bag, the wolf girl closes it, saying, "Well, this'll have to do for now. Let's get back before-" As she turns, her nose touches a floating puffball.

All their attention on the harvesting of the young fungus, no one noticed the puffball closing in on them from behind. With a subtle pop, a cloud of rust colored dust coats the two canines' faces. The others immediately leap away calling the girls' names in distress. Twinkaleni warns them not to breathe it in, but it's too late, they both inhale in surprise and begin to cough. The density of the spores makes Alice's throat go dry as she waves the cloud away. Lyca kneels to Nesu, who was also caught in the cloud, to blow and brush some of the powder from his light tan fur.

Philip shakes his head, "Oh no, we, we have to get back, we need the cure!"

Danahlia approaches Alice only to have Lyca growl, "No! Nobody get near us!" She then dusts off the fungi filled sack and tosses it to Philip, "Take the others back to camp and get that tea brewin'."

Philip catches it, "But Lyca-"

"Go!" Lyca orders, "We'll catch up."

"Alice?" Twinkaleni calls, as the others head back.

"Go on, I'll be fine," Alice assures, "We'll meet back at their camp."

Danahlia puts her tail around the Murin mage, urging her on while waving back, "We'll save you a cup!"

Once the others have left them, Lyca continues to clean off a frightened Nesu, "We have to get as much of this stuff off us as we can."

Alice rubs at her face and pats at her fur, releasing a thin haze of spores, but after a moment her dry throat prompts her to take a drink from a waterskin. The forest dwellers hadn't been carrying any water and she offers the skin to Lyca. The wolf girl accepts it with a grim smile.

She lets Nesu have a drink before taking any herself, and then returns it, "Thanks, you're all right, Red. Sorry about earlier, with the whole stealin' your sword thing. Where'd you get that anyway?"

"My dad left it for me," Alice replies, recorking her waterskin.

"He fightin' in the war?"

"He... was. He isn't anymore."

Her tone must have conveyed the message because Lyca's tapered, tan ears droop, "Oh, sorry."

"Don't be, I figure it's the same for everyone else in your gang," says Alice, brushing off an arm.

"Gang, huh?" the wolf girl smirks to Nesu, the tiny Murin smiling as she cleans his fur, "Yeah, that's about right."

Curious and a little worried about their predicament, Alice asks, "Has anyone... died? From the sickness?"

"Oh, no, no," Lyca is quick to say, "But, uh, no one's gotten better either."

"Mmm," Alice groans.

"Yeah. We're really hopin' that Murin friend o' yours knows what she's talkin' about."

Alice assures the pair that she does, hoping its true herself. After a time, Alice squats behind Lyca and begins brushing and blowing away the dirty orange spores from her fur much like she sees her doing to Nesu. The wolf girl glides her tail along Alice's calves thankfully. It's a slow process, but eventually Nesu and Lyca are relatively spore free. Lyca returns the favor, brushing away the spores from Alice's fur, while Nesu does his part in dusting her off as well, though in doing so, he ends up with more spores on him.

Alice asks about the quite boy and Lyca tells her that when she found him he was wandering the streets in a small town. The Murin says he has many brothers and sisters but no father. Lyca theorizes that his mother may have abandoned him in favor of trying to keep his other siblings fed.

"But you fit right in with us, don't cha, buddy?" the wolf girl says, giving the newly cleaned Murin a hug. Nesu hugs her back, rubbing his soft furred head into her chest.

The trio begins the walk back, being cautious of anymore floating puffballs. With the smaller group, they're easier to avoid. Not long into their walk, Lyca spots a snake resting in a beam of sunlight coiled high around a tree's trunk. It's easily as thick as Alice's thigh and long enough to wrap around the thick tree several times, but high enough up that it doesn't pose an immediate threat. It's brown for the most part and blends in well with the bark of the tree though its head is hidden somewhere behind a branch.

"Ooo, let's get it," Lyca bubbles excitedly.

"What, why? How?" asks Alice, the Lobovan licking her lips in anticipation.

"Look at all that meat! We can't just leave it there," points out Lyca, reminding Alice very much of Danahlia.

"It's big," puts in Nesu.

"You said it. We can eat off that for a day at least."

Alice eyes the massive snake, "But how are we gonna get it? Is it poisonous?"

She had little experience with snakes but knew they were largely to be avoided because of the potential for a venomous bite. This was by far the largest such creature she had ever seen.

"Nah, it's a constrictor, only a problem if it wraps around you. So, you know, don't let it do that," advises Lyca, still too excited about the encounter for Alice's taste.

"Ok," says Alice with little enthusiasm, "So, how do we get it down?"

"Let *me* worry about that. You go hide in the bushes and be ready. Nesu, go with 'er and watch 'er back."

"But-" Nesu whines.

"No buts, she doesn't know the forest like we do, you gotta protect her, go go go," says Lyca, giving the tiny boy a push in Alice's direction. He reluctantly approaches Alice and they pick a bush to crouch behind. Through it, they watch Lyca announce, a dramatic hand to her forehead, "Ugh, I can't go on. I'm done for." The wolf girl then falls to her side, tail wagging.

The snake doesn't react at all.

After a minute her tail slows to a stop and she peeks up at the unresponsive reptile before wailing, "Oh! It's so unfortunate that a delicious meal, such as myself, would perish in this way, alone, in the woods, defenseless." She then rolls to her back, spread eagle, with her tongue hanging from her mouth.

Alice, unsure what to think, asks the Murin boy, "Has, she done this before?"

Nesu gives his head a quick shake before worriedly looking on. After another minute, Lyca peaks from under a hand to the snake, a tapered ear angling toward it. The snake hasn't budged an inch. She then reaches for a rock and throws it at the snake, hitting the trunk just below its coils, shouting, "Hey! Free food!"

The snake's body doesn't move but its head comes from around the branch to peer at Lyca, long black forked tongue flicking in irritation. The wolf girl immediately begins a pathetic crawl as if both her legs were useless. After maybe two feet, she collapses back into stillness. The snake watches for a time, suspiciously, if snakes can be suspicious, before very slowly making its way down the tree. It stops frequently to eye Lyca, who peeks at it without moving.

Once on the ground, the snake gathers the rest of its lengthy body before moving closer to the prone wolf girl. The snake's head is kept lifted from the ground while it slithers over to its prey as if examining the Lobovan, its tongue flickering out rapidly.

"Anytime, Red," Lyca calls as the snake gets within a few feet of her and she begins to shift uncomfortably. The snake recoils at her movement, tucking back into itself and hissing angrily, revealing many sharp teeth. Alice takes her cue and charges as silently as she can for the thick serpent's flank.

"Now would be good!" Lyca shouts, crawling away from the menacing snake as it rapidly moves in.

It senses Alice's attack and looks to her, but the Tokala brings her sword down hard in an overhead chop that severs it two feet below its head. Despite being cut in two, the snake trashes about wildly on the ground, baring its array of backward facing teeth. Alice manages to remove it's head while Nesu leaps on the wiggling tail end, biting at it repeatedly until it stills.

"Nice one," Lyca comments as she gets to her feet and dusts herself off.

The fox girl lets out a breath, "It's Alice, by the way."

Lyca passes her with a negligent, "Uh-huh," and then to Nesu exclaims, "Wow, you really saved my tail there buddy," while pulling the weakly coiling snake away from him.

The little mouse stands over the snake breathing heavily, glaring at it as if daring it to move again. Lyca gives him a big hug and he beams, a little blood staining the fur around his mouth and down his neck.

"How can so much brave be packed into such a little guy?" she coos to the Murin.

Sighing, Alice cuts the snake's body into two more halves and as she does, Jellybane begins to glow.

"Whoa, what's with that?" asks Lyca, pointing to the luminous, green blade.

Alice grins, "Yeah, it does that sometimes. It's enchanted."

Nesu, mesmerized by the sword's magic, reaches out for it only to have Lyca grab his hand, "No, Nesu, that's sharp," she gives his fingers a squeeze, "Ouch."

The mouse boy frowns but Alice lets them watch the sword glow brighter as the snake blood dries and flakes away from its keen edge, leaving it spotless. After Nesu is cleaned up, they each grab a length of snake, the small Murin taking the shortest chunk while Lyca and Alice drape the larger pieces over their shoulders for the trip back to the forest dweller's camp.

As they walk, Alice tells them about her previous adventure in the forest near her hometown. She goes over how she met Danahlia and Twinkaleni, the trouble in Toki, the pixies, and all their battles with monsters. Nesu is enthralled by the tale, asking over and over, "Then what happened?" though Lyca seems less impressed.

It's late in the afternoon when the trio nears the camp and they can hear the others hustling about.

A young Lagomorph carrying branches spots them and shouts, "Hey, they're back! Lyca and Nesu are back!"

The brown furred rabbit girl jogs toward them as calls further back relay the message. Soon most of those well enough to walk, including Danahlia and Twinkaleni, are there to welcome them.

"Look at you, the big game hunter!" greets Danahlia happily.

"Ali, Alice, are you alright?" Twinkaleni huffs.

"Yeah, fine," Alice says, letting Danahlia take the length of snake from her, "What happened to you?"

Danahlia answers for the breathless little mouse girl, "Twinkie managed to get a fire goin'."

"Really? But the wood around here is so damp," says Alice, surprised.

Danahlia grins down at the mage, "Yup. Got everybody gettin' wood to keep it goin', don't think she, oop-" Danahlia catches Twinkaleni against her leg as she topples over, "There she goes again."

Alice picks up the unconscious Murin, letting her head rest over one shoulder, and they all head back to the heart of the camp.

After giving Philip her load of snake, Lyca, comes up to Alice and asks, "What happened to your friend?"

"Using magic takes a bit out of her and she used a lot today," Alice replies, cradling the small girl in her arms.

"Huh. They're sayin' she got a fire goin' and that the fungus tea is brewin'. Plus we got this huge snake to chow on, so," Lyca looks away, "you guys should stick around."

Alice looks to the Lobovan with a smirk, "Are you inviting us to be part o' your gang?"

Lyca puts up her hands, "Whoa, hey, nobody said that. I'm just sayin', while you're in the forest, maybe we work together."

"Yeah, I guess you guys can tag along with us for a little bit," says Danahlia laying down the snake beside where Philip set down the hunk he received from Lyca.

Lyca makes an irritated noise with her lips, "Like we'd need *you*. We been doin' just fine before you showed up."

Danahlia barks a laugh, "Ha! You already needed us a whole bunch today and we just met."

"You know what?!" Lyca shoots back as Philip gets in between the two, trying to placate them.

Alice decides to stay out of it and feels wise for doing so. She instead examines the fire Twinkaleni somehow started. It cracks and sizzles with wisps of steam fuming from the broken ends of damp branches but is nonetheless going strong. Someone's set the iron pot the girls bought in Carton over it. The heating water within slowly mixes with the fungus to make what they all hope will be the cure for the sickness. The rabbit girl from before offers a place for Alice to lay Twinkaleni down, but for now she chooses to hold onto her.

As the tea brews and forest dwellers drop off the driest leaves and branches they can find in a pile near the fire, Alice sits down holding the Murin mage in her lap. She pets Twinkaleni's soft, fine fur wondering how someone so tiny and adorable could have such incredible power. The smaller girl's breathing reaches a more relaxed pace and Alice gives her a hug.

Apparently done with her spat with Lyca, Danahlia asks from behind, "How's she doin'?"

"Good, I think. Just needs to rest 'o bit," replies Alice, smiling.

"Wags. Mind if I borrow Jellybane? Everybody's waiting to get this guy on the fire," the Liguna says, hooking a thumb at the snake.

"Yeah, sure."

Alice feels the weight on her back lighten as Danahlia draws her sword. She then sets Twinkaleni down on a bed of grass, giving her a last pet on the head before watching Danahlia clean the snake. The lizard girl proudly shows Alice the skins she gets off the pieces before removing the guts and then cutting the meat into U shaped chunks of a few ribs each. Alice begins to smell a heavy earthy scent and looks to see that the tea is bubbling with little bits of the fungus floating to the top.

She turns to ask Danahlia for her spear and sees several of the forest children gathered around the Liguna, watching in awe as Jellybane glows bright to rid itself of snake entrails once more.

Danahlia swells from the attention and looks back to Alice with a wide grin when she calls, "Danny, I think the tea's ready. Let's get it off the fire."

The lizard girl rushes over with her spear in one hand and Jellybane in the other, giving Alice the latter. She then puts the haft of her spear through the looped handles of the iron pot, lifts it off the fire, and sets it on the ground to cool. The children gather around, murmuring their excitement over finally being able to help their friends.

"Ok, ok, it's going to be a while before its cool enough to drink. Meanwhile, the fire's free, let's get some food cookin'!" Philip announces to happy cheers.

Sticks are put through bits of snake and mushrooms while various tubers are placed beside the fire to cook and hopefully soften. The sacks of picked greens and berries are passed around and everyone grabs a hand full to munch on. Alice doesn't find the leaves particularly appetizing but mixed with the occasional saccha berry and her own hunger, she eagerly eats and grabs more when the sacks pass again. Somehow the greens only make her feel even hungrier and she, like many of the others, eagerly waits for the snake to cook.

The serpent's light pink meat turns pale, almost white, as it cooks and, along with the mushrooms, smells wonderful. Danahlia becomes impatient and tries to bite into one of the pieces cooking on the tip of her spear. She lets out a cry, finding it far too hot and begins fanning her tongue, much to the amusement of the others. Alice pulls away her own and brings it to her nose, feeling the warmth radiating off of it and smelling the sweet scent. Mouth already watering, she takes the time to blow on it before having a bite. She moans in pleasure as her teeth sink into the tender flesh, hot juices dripping to her tongue. Pulling the meat from the bone, she sees Lyca doing the same and they share a smile, greatly enjoying the meal and the company.

A second round of snake is being put over the fire when Twinkaleni comes to sit between Danahlia and Alice. She sleepily rubs her eyes and yawns as Danahlia greets, "Hey! Look who's up. How ya feelin'?"

"Ravenous," Twinkaleni replies.

"Good, good, here," Danahlia grins, handing her a cooked piece of snake.

The mouse girl accepts the meat, gives it a sniff, and then begins nibbling on it. Philip comes up to the trio and kneels before them, "You really saved us today. We're all grateful, thank you."

The girls give him a warm smile, Twinkaleni having bits of meat stuck between her two front teeth.

Lyca is blowing over the steaming pot with several others. Looking over at Philip she says, "Don't start prayin' to 'em just yet. We still don't know if this tea's gonna work."

Unfazed and smiling brightly, the Echanian replies, "Maybe, but there is a chance, and that gives us hope. Somethin' we've not had in a while."

By the time everyone has had something to eat, the tea is cool enough to try. Danahlia offers one of her empty waterskins and they carefully fill it with the steaming brew. The first swallows are given to those who have been sick the longest until it reaches Lyca, Nesu, and Alice. Alice finds the tea tastes remarkably like liquid dirt. Everyone who had been exposed to the puffball spores is given a mouth full but the pot is empty before a second can go all the way around.

Tipping the pot to get the last lingering drops, Lyca asks, "How much o' this stuff are we supposed to drink?"

"I'm not sure," admits Twinkaleni, peering at the back page of the entry, "It only says the tea will help alleviate the symptoms. There is no mention of the necessary quantity or time it will take to recover."

"We should try to find more fungus then. Keep makin' more tea until everyone's better," suggests Philip.

"I agree, and I have a few ideas that might make our search easier," Twinkaleni adds.

Chapter 8

Fall of a King

The next morning, Alice wakes with a dry, itchy throat. Drinking soothes it a bit but only for a while. She's rubbing the fur along her neck, causing a prickly sensation in her esophagus, when Lyca joins her by the shrinking pool.

"That's how it starts," says the wolf girl, getting a drink herself.

It's still very early and only a few of the forest dwellers are up, though the fire has been tended to all night. Keeping her voice low, Alice asks, "What?"

"The sickness, that tingling in the back o' your throat that won't go away. That's how it started for everyone."

"But we drank the tea," Alice reasons, her worry growing.

Lyca shrugs, "Who knows if it'll work."

"Maybe we just need more," Alice suggests, getting another drink of water.

The two take over looking after the fire so the last two attendees can sleep. They break branches into long sticks, setting the smaller pieces into the flames, as the duo before them did. A few of the tougher roots and tubers from yesterday are in the iron pot slowly boiling with a few greens and much of what's left of the snake. Alice feels a little hungry, but the group agreed this would be left for those unable to walk. True, she had a some food stored in her pack, but feels it would be smarter to keep it for more desperate times. After all, they were hunting today.

As more of the group wake, they have a small breakfast of leftovers while going over the plans from last night. Twelve, including Alice, Twinkaleni, and Danahlia, plan to head out into the forest. They have several goals. The first is to test an idea Twinkaleni had for dealing with the floating puffballs. If successful, they will forage and hunt, all the while trying to clear a path back to the forest dweller's abandoned camp. Reclaiming the camp will give Alice and her companions a good staging point to resume their journey through the thick forest while also greatly aiding Lyca and Philip's group. They all know it will be a risky trip, but the forest dwellers are especially eager to get on with it. Success will mean healing their friends and getting back their home.

The twelve prepare, Alice, Twinkaleni, and Danahlia, taking all their belongings, while Lyca, Philip, and the older brother of the Lagomorph girl, place the ends of the long sticks into the fire. Once they're lit, the forest dwellers carry a bundle of them, keeping the tips close together so their collective heat keeps them burning. Others carry sacks and simple wooden spears. Once the party is ready, they set out.

As they walk, Alice sharpens a few of the group's spears, giving them finer points. She has managed a few when they spot their first floating puffball. Philip steps up to take this one and hands his bundle of burning sticks to another, keeping one for the task. The puffball is drifting slowly by, three feet off the ground. Philip blows on the burning end of the stick, the embers there glowing brighter until a small flame appears. He then slowly and carefully extends the stick below the puffball.

"Remember to let only the flame touch it, not the stick," Twinkaleni reminds anxiously, her tiny arms squeezing her book.

Focused on the effort, Philip manages to keep the stick's flame lit while reaching out as far as he can to avoid any spores. He needn't worry. One of the long hairs hanging off the puffball drifts near enough to catch and, like the fuse to a bomb, quickly carries the flame to its host causing it to erupt in a bright ball of fire. It's noisy but by now the group knows what to expect and only cheers their success. Finally, they had a way to fight back.

As planned, from here the twelve split into four groups of three. Twinkaleni advised this to increase the chances of finding immature fungi for the cure, cover more ground for potential forage, and widen the safe route to the forest dwellers' camp. Philip, Twinkaleni, and Danahlia form one group, while Alice goes with Lyca and Nesu. They wish each other well and begin to fan out. As the distance between groups widens, the pops of more detonated puffballs encourages them all on.

Alice spots an older puffball fungal formation on the trunk of a still living tree and accepts one of the burning sticks from Lyca. Twinkaleni had destroyed these with her fire spell, but the sticks were yet untested. Alice blows on the end of the stick until a faint flame ignites at the tip and then pokes the fungus. At the point of contact, sizzling embers bloom and spread in a fine orange wave across the entire splatter leaving it black. Once it's done, Alice scratches the charred fungus with the stick to find it's become little more than ash.

"That was easy," grins Alice.

"Alright," Lyca says approvingly, "I guess your friend knows a thing or two."

The trio venture more boldly into the forest, taking turns popping the floating puffballs and burning away their parent fungi. The echoing pops of floaters elsewhere let them know the other groups are progressing as well. The frequent explosions are no doubt keeping ferals away but the small group does manage to gather a descent bit of forage now that they no longer have to fear the floating puffballs. After a time they come across a tree with a thick round canopy that has fruit Lyca calls deliduss.

The deliduss fruit are shaped similarly to apples, but have a subtle bumpy texture to their skin. Some of the fruit are just becoming ripe, turning a bright orange, while many are still yellow and even green. Alice, Lyca, and Nesu, pick one each to try and find it sweet and tangy. The fruit has a crunch to it but still yields easily to Alice's teeth. Like the apple it resembles, the core contains several small seeds. They toss these into the surrounding forest with the hope that they might germinate into more such trees. After their snack, the group begins carefully picking the rest of the ripe fruit. They have to be cautious doing this because the branches of the deliduss tree have long, thin thorns, sparse but well hidden among lush leaves.

Once they get all they can reach, Nesu circling around the lowest branches while Lyca and Alice bag any around the middle, Alice stands on Lyca's back to reach even higher. They trade off who is on all fours and who picks as they ring the tree.

Lyca is on Alice's back when Nesu announces excitedly, "Lyca, I smell aphy juice."

"What?" asks Alice, her arms shaking under the wolf girl's weight.

"Ok, we'll go get it in a sec," says Lyca, her toes nails digging uncomfortably into the Tokala's shoulder.

"It's over here!" squeaks the Murin as he sniffs the air and heads into the trees.

Alice, gritting her teeth, watches him go, "He's runnin' off."

"Nesu! No, wait!" Lyca shouts, her weight shifting on Alice's back.

She makes an annoyed sound and it feels like she hops, nearly planting Alice's face into the earth. The Tokala manages to hold out, hearing the sound of the tree shake as the Lobovan plucks one last fruit before getting off of her.

Alice rolls onto her back in relief and, upside down, watches Lyca run after the little mouse boy calling, "Come on, Red!"

Grumbling, Alice gets to her feet, picks up her sword, and, stretching her back, jogs after them.

She finds the pair only a short distance away, Lyca kneeling before Nesu, admonishing him for leaving without her.

The mouse boy whines, "But it was right here," pointing to a bulbous plant near the ground among large, wide, green leaves.

As Nesu endures a scolding, Alice looks closer at the strange plant. It resembles a melon, oblong in shape, standing on the ground so it's taller than it is wide. It's lime green save for the top where the color changes to a bright red at a wide opening. An interestingly enticing smell is coming from it, something like fresh fruit.

"Is this what he wanted?" Alice asks, seeing the top opening has a hairy lip curving outward along the rim.

"Mm-hm," sniffles Nesu.

"Yeah, it's an amphora plant," says Lyca, the two approaching.

"It smells," Alice takes a deep inhale through her nose, lured closer to the opening, "good."

Lyca grins, "Look inside, but don't touch it."

Alice does, finding the melon thing is filled about halfway with some kind of clear liquid, the delicious fruity scent growing stronger.

"Aphy juice," supplies Nesu.

"You drink it?" Alice asks, tempted to put her hand in to scoop some up.

"Yup, good stuff, but don't touch the lip. Here, let me," Lyca approaches with her spear and seems intent on piercing the plant near its base. Nesu holds out his hands, cupped in eager anticipation just below Lyca's spear point, but then the Lobovan looks back to Alice, "Any o' your waterskins empty?"

One nearly is and they share what's left before letting Nesu hold it open right under where Lyca punctures the melon shaped bulb. She twists the point of her spear into the apparently soft flesh of the plant until the clear liquid comes streaming out. Nesu catches it in the waterskin until the plant is empty, then immediately takes a drink. He lets out a delighted noise when he swallows, offering the skin to Lyca. She takes a drink, grins, and gives the skin back to Alice. She sniffs at it, the tantalizing scent's obvious source, and takes a drink too.

The juice is warm, sweet, thin like water, and delicious. It leaves a tingling sensation on Alice's tongue that makes her stick it out to see the cause though there's nothing there. Lyca laughs taking another drink before passing it to Nesu. In good spirits they continue on, burning away the puffballs and gathering what they can, eyes open for the immature fungi.

By late afternoon, the trio finally arrives in the forest dweller's main camp, the first to do so. Alice figures they must have been here for some time because they'd set up a few makeshift huts from sticks and woven branches. The simple structures are set in an expanding circle in front of a cave.

Excited to be back, Nesu scampers off toward the cave as Lyca sets down her forage sack and bundle of sticks to throw open her arms, "Well, what do ya think? Not too shabby huh?"

Alice sets down her things, relieved they finally made it. She peers around noting rotting bedrolls made of woven grasses, a couple of fire pits with a few battered earthen wares around them, and a fallen tree trunk that might serve as a bench or even a table.

"It needs a little fixin' up o' course. It's been a while and we had to leave in kind of a hurry," the wolf girl admits.

Alice takes one of the burning sticks, nearly half the original length now, and pops a floating puffball drifting lazily by, before grinning, "Wags."

Lyca smiles, pointing, "There's a pond just over there. We should probably-"

Nesu lets out a panicked squeak and comes flying out of the cave toward them, the boy crying, "Monster, monster!"

Alice draws her sword and Lyca takes up her spear as he hides behind her legs, all eyes on the dark cave mouth. Alice picks up a subtle taping, rapid and continuous, each individual tap blending in with a score of others to make one long rattling sound that grows louder with each second. The tapping reaches its apex when two long, yellow sticks come waving out from the shadows, rapping at the ground but too slowly, too cautiously, to be the source of the noise. Alice's grip on her sword tightens and her teeth clench as the yellow sticks get longer and thicker, reaching out from the cave to become the antennas of some kind of gigantic multi-legged worm.

Its antennas are easily as big around as Alice's arms at their base and wave around independent of each other from the front of a bright orange head. Shiny and rounded, it's about as wide as Alice's torso. The head is quickly followed by a segmented body of similar color and proportions, though these segments instead have legs the same color as the antennas. The creature seems hesitant to come out of the cave, sticking to the shadows until it can gather more of itself. This takes some time as more and more legged segments appear from the darkness to curl around the previous.

A chill runs through the young Tokala as she sees how absurdly long it is. Her tail tucks, ears fall back, and grip loosens as her nerve crumbles. She looks to Lyca to see if she intends flight or fight. The wolf girl's eyes widen and her mouth opens steadily as she looks on. The head of the goliath creature swings around uncertainly and then freezes, its antennas standing straight out toward the trio. Suddenly, it rushes them with unexpected speed, head low, lengthy body following.

"Oh, ticks," Lyca lets out breathlessly.

Alice, terrified and strangely fascinated, watches as the creature closes on them. Its legs work in a wave to propel the enormous thing. Lyca shifts to her right, pulling her attention away from their attacker.

The Lobovan pushes Nesu away from her and hurriedly tells him, "Run, find the others, GO!"

Startled by Lyca's shout, the Murin freezes for a second before fleeing for the trees the same way they had come.

Alice wonders if they should split up, running in different directions to avoid all being eaten by the monster, but before she can say anything Lyca snarls, "We had to run once, but this is *my* home and I'm takin' it BACK!"

The Lobovan charges the giant with her wooden spear.

"Lyca!" Alice shouts, torn between fleeing after the mouse and aiding the crazed wolf girl. Her body shifts as if intending to go backward and forward at the same time, but her feet stay still, legs shaking. Knowing she'd hate herself for the rest of her life if she abandoned her new friend, Alice raises Jellybane over her head and charges in too, screaming.

Lyca gets within a few feet of the oncoming monster before using her spear to vault herself over it. The orange giant lifts its head to track her, revealing two thick, curved mandibles spanning wide to take the wolf girl. An opening made, Alice leaps in to deliver a hard vertical chop aimed at splitting the creature down the middle. But it shifts, turning to follow Lyca to its back, causing her blow to only sever several thick legs on its right side before glancing off a hard carapace. The monster jerks in rage as it turns back toward Alice, knocking the fox girl several feet to its side. Alice tumbles to the ground but works it into a roll and catches herself, winded but not injured.

The massive worm can't turn sharply enough to get at her without making a wide arc and Alice uses the precious seconds to look for her sword, having lost it in the fall. She spots the gleaming blade under the bug, almost being trampled by its many legs as it maneuvers around for another attack. Looking back to see the creature's front end nearly upon her, she knows she won't be able to reach Jellybane in time. Then there's Lyca, straddling the monster while futilely stabbing at it with her spear, the wooden point breaking on the durable shell.

"Lyca! My sword!" shouts Alice, pointing for a split second before she needs to run from the oncoming bug's mandibles.

Lyca sees it and as she passes by, she holds onto the monster's thick body with her legs and leans over the side, taking up the enchanted weapon. Alice runs parallel to the long insect toward the cave, forcing it into a U before leaping over its body near the end to get on its opposite side. Meanwhile, Lyca plunges Jellybane down into the giant, the sharp, steel blade penetrating deep.

The effect is immediate, the monster worm writhing, its body trying to turn in onto itself. Lyca tumbles off, rolling to Alice's side and the Tokala helps the Lobovan to her feet, Jellybane still in the creature. They step away to watch as the giant wiggles wildly as if trying to reach the sword in its back. After some struggle, Jellybane begins to glow green but this time the blade brightens far more than usual until the squirming bug simply breaks in two where the sword pierces it, an acrid burning smell permeating the air. The greater portion of the bug stills, but the half with the head continues to move, pulling away from its dead end to target the girls.

Even missing several legs, the monster moves swiftly toward them, antennae pointing accusingly.

"Oh, that is just not fair!" Lyca groans as Alice shouts for them to run. They both turn and take off into the trees, the giant bug in hot pursuit.

As they flee, Lyca huffs, "There should be a rule! If you cut somethin' in half, it should die!"

"Tell it that!" Alice calls back, trying to come up with a plan.

Lyca bares her teeth and shouts over her shoulder, "Hey! You're supposed to be dead!"

Alice gives her a glance, feet pounding the moist earth, and then she has it.

"Split up, circle around, he can only chase one of us, the other gets the sword!" she gasps between rapid breaths.

Lyca nods and veers off to the right while Alice turns left. The monster follows Lyca. Alice dashes back to the camp to search for Jellybane, instead finding Danahlia, Twinkaleni, Philip, and Nesu looking at the dead half of the giant bug.

"Guys!" she rasps and begins to cough, her throat terribly dry.

"Hey," Danahlia grins as they turn to her, "Looks like we missed the party."

Alice shakes her head, trying to breathe between coughs.

Twinkaleni looks puzzled, "Alice? Are you alright?"

Nesu looks about nervously, calling out, "Lyca? Lyca?!"

"Where is she?" asks Philip.

Alice manages to point in the direction she last saw the wolf girl, gasping, "Big. Bug," she then points at the still half, "Coming. Not dead."

This alerts them and Danahlia pokes her spear at the severed half, "This thing is still alive?"

Alice nods and then points more urgently in the direction Lyca was running.

She sees Jellybane and starts toward it when Lyca bursts from the trees, crying, "Get it get it get it get it get it!"

The Lobovan dashes across the camp and then starts weaving around trees and huts, trying desperately to widen the narrowing gap between her and the shockingly fast, bisected monster. The others are taken off guard and simply stare for a few seconds, trying to grasp the situation. Then Philip lifts one side of the log sitting in the middle of the camp and shouts to Lyca, "Over here!"

Lyca turns toward him and is clearly nearing the end of her stamina when she dives by. As the bug nears, the Echanian's muscles flex hard as he throws his side of the log into the bug's path with a grunt. It almost slips under but the weight of the log comes down on the creature's back, pinning it in place with a loud crack of its brittle carapace. Philip has to jump away to avoid its thrashing head when it tries to bite him. Then Danahlia ends the massive worm with a carefully aimed thrust from her spear.

"Ticks, what *is* this thing?" Danahlia asks, lifting its head with her still embedded spear to see its mandibles.

"Monster," Nesu states as if it should be obvious.

The little mouse is kneeling at Lyca's side, the wolf girl herself on her back, breathing raggedly in between dry coughs. Alice nods, drinking from the waterskin offered to her by Twinkaleni. Philip, after making sure the monster isn't playing opossum, checks on the Lobovan too.

The Murin mage offers the skin to Lyca once Alice is done, then, looking over at the dead, multi legged worm, says, "I believe it is known as a Greater King Centipede. There is an entry of just such a creature in my book, though seeing the illustration provides little preparation for an actual encounter with such a monstrosity."

Alice recovers Jellybane and examines the cut that divided the giant. The great wounds have been cauterized, black and gray ash sealing them with bits of transparent, yolk colored goo seeping out where the bug's insides leak. She looks down at her deceptively simple broadsword wondering what else it might be able to do.

Twinkaleni appears beside her, "Did you do all this?"

"No, it was Jellybane. It cut the monster in half," Alice whispers, still having trouble believing it.

"Remarkable," the little Murin intones, picking at the brittle, burnt edges of the centipede's bisected body.

"Wonder how his majesty tastes," chimes Danahlia, removing her spear for its head.

"As I recall, the text *did* say it was edible," mentions Twinkaleni.

The groups put what remains of their bundled sticks together in one of the camp's fire pits and, after a little coaxing, have a small fire going. They are soon joined by the other six, who are happy to report that they've found more of the immature fungi for the healing tea. Even though it's getting late, Philip decides to take a group back to their other camp in order to prepare the sick for the journey tomorrow. He and his party are given most of the fungi and a generous portion of the food the groups have gathered today in the hopes it will give the ill forest dwellers the strength to make the trip. Meanwhile, Lyca, Nesu, Alice, Twinkaleni, Danahlia and two others, stay behind to secure the camp and prepare for their arrival.

Danahlia and two forest dwellers hunt for potential fire wood while Lyca takes Alice and Twinkaleni to the cave. The inside is quite dry, if dark, and is where the forest dwellers stored much of their food and supplies. Though the centipede, and no doubt other scavengers, have eaten what was left, Lyca finds her group's cache of utensils relatively intact. Nesu picks out a small pot that should be perfect for brewing tea and hands it to Lyca, earning a pat on the head, while Alice finds a bow and arrows.

"Wow, where'd you get these?" she asks, picking the wooden bow up. It looks well made from a single piece of wood, rather than cobbled together like hers was.

Lyca smirks, "Like that huh? The Cold Blood pair I told you about left it for us before they took off. There's another one around here somewhere..."

"Estraleete," calls Twinkaleni, a small ball of ember light forming between her palms.

The cave now lit, Lyca gives the mage an approving, "Huh, you just got all kinds a tricks don't cha?"

Twinkaleni grins and then shifts away as a mesmerized Nesu reaches for the light. Not much larger than the boy, Twinkaleni can't keep it from him and the moment one of his outstretched fingers touches the little ball, it vanishes.

Nesu lets out a sad, "Oh."

Twinkaleni quickly summons another, chiding, "Now, you must be careful. Light can be a fragile element. It can be bent and even broken by the slightest touch."

Having learned his lesson, Nesu puts his hands around his back and follows Twinkaleni around as the group searches for anything they might need. Now that they can see the whole of it, the main chamber of the cave is not very deep but wide and cluttered with everything from torn sacks, which may have held food, various leaves, more woven beds, sticks, clay or wooden bowls, and even some rudimentary tools.

"What's that?" Alice asks, pointing to an unusual configuration of sticks that have been tied together.

"Oh, that's the bow we were tryin' to make. The Cold Bloods taught us how to build 'em so we were givin' it a go. That one should be about done now," says Lyca, picking up a knife. She places the knife in a large clay pot, picks it up and also takes the sticks before leading them back outside to the fire.

Danahlia has managed to get the flames to a less precarious height and now stands by the remains of the king centipede, scraping away at the ash left by Jellybane with her claws. She recoils when a puffy yellow clump pushes free from where she had been picking as it were under pressure. The lizard girl then sniffs at it before sticking out her fleshy, pink tongue to lick it. Alice and the others watch in a mix of curiosity and disgust.

Danahlia notices them staring at her and grins, "Not bad, might be better if we cook it though."

The others come to investigate as Danahlia tears away the clump and gives it a few squeezes. It seems mushy but retains its shape when released like a sponge. The Liguna tries to skewer it on a stick but it plops off back into her hand. Lyca blows dust from the inside of her clay pot before offering it and Danahlia drops the bug meat inside with a wet little splat. Using her claws, Danahlia removes more of the burnt flesh and scoops out great handfuls of the yellow mush, steadily filling the pot. While she does, Alice and the others take up burning sticks to scour the camp and surrounding woods for any more puffballs as well as to collect more wood before it gets dark.

Alice finds a couple of the older fungal splatters and turns them to ash. Hearing the now familiar pops elsewhere lets her know that there are still some puffballs floating about. She looks around for a time but doesn't see any herself. The sun is setting, causing shadows to deepen. This and unfamiliar sounds are making her more and more eager to return to her friends. The young Tokala picks up the thick end of a large fallen branch and hurriedly drags it back to camp.

When she arrives, Danahlia is stirring the clay pot with a thick stick. As Alice's branch rustles behind her, Danahlia looks up and calls, "Hey, check this out."

The Liguna pulls free the stick to show a clump of steaming centipede meat stuck to the other end, though it looks different. Alice lets go of the branch and steps closer to investigate. The meat now looks more like dough swirled around the end of the stick. It's thick enough that Danahlia only has to turn the stick a little to keep it from dropping off.

"Did you try it?" Alice asks, smelling the warm pleasant scent of cooked food.

"Yeah, it's good. Here," Danahlia replies, holding it out to her.

Alice accepts it and looks to see Twinkaleni sitting with Nesu on one of the old woven bedrolls, already enjoying her own centipede on a stick. Alice blows on the steaming pale yellow clump and watches the lizard girl scoop up some more from the centipede to plop it into the pot before she sets it back over the fire. Alice moves to join Twinkaleni and sees her take a bite. It's amusing to see the little Murin try to blow and chew at the same time, little puffs of steam drifting from her mouth. Grumbling stomach uninterested in waiting anymore, Alice tries it too.

Aside from being very hot, the bug meat is soft and moist, having the sticky texture of the dough it resembles. Alice doesn't get a chance to taste it, instead letting the chunk drop from her mouth before it can scorch her tongue anymore.

"It's hot," Nesu informs her, looking up from Twinkaleni's book.

"Thankth," says Alice, her tongue hanging out.

Nesu looks at her, wide eyed, for a moment before being drawn back to the book. While the mage eats, he flips through a few pages until he finds something he likes and then points, "What's that?"

Twinkaleni swallows a mouthful before reading, "Carbuncle, an elusive creature seen only once in all my travels, and then, only for an instant, but its beauty will stay with me to the end of my days. Spotted in the mountains of Abaharran near some old mines, it was roughly the size of a coney but with features more akin to a feral... cat," she reads, angling her book toward the flames to see the page better. Something occurs to her and she sets the book in Nesu's lap before making her way to her pack, rummaging around in it.

"You let him hold your book but you won't even let me touch it? I thought we were better than that, Twinkie," Danahlia calls, as she makes another bug pop for a young Houdain.

"Indeed," Twinkaleni replies without looking at her, "Nesu has an appreciation for the acquisition of knowledge that you seem to lack."

Danahlia sticks her tongue out at the mage.

"Ah, here it is," Twinkaleni chimes as she pulls free the enchanted core stone, its green light bright in the surrounding darkness. As she makes her way back to sit beside Nesu, he dutifully places his hands around his back, watching the core stone with undisguised interest. Twinkaleni tries to slide the book back into her lap but unable to handle her food, the book, and stone, she offers the glowing orb to Nesu. He immediately reaches for it but stops himself and looks curiously to Twinkaleni.

"It's alright, you can hold this one," she says, "Just don't drop it."

The younger Murin takes the core, looking deep into the mysterious light. It's bright enough that Twinkaleni can read, so she continues, "It had great ears that made me think it could fly if it chose and a marvelous coat of aqua marine. From what I could gather, the folk around say it takes gems from the mines. Some say catching a Carbuncle will bring you good luck, others say bad. Never bought into superstition myself."

Nesu asks what superstition is and Twinkaleni explains as Alice looks at the image beside the entry. It does look like a cat, though with longer limbs and massive wing like ears. Its tail too is thick and bushy, not so dissimilar from her own. Its eyes are almond shaped with a squat muzzle like a feline.

"What's the next one?" the young Houdain asks.

Surprised, Alice looks around to see almost everyone, including Lyca, has gathered around, perhaps drawn by the core stone or Twinkaleni's reading, though probably a little of both. It makes her smile and she tries the bug meat again.

It's cool enough now and the outside has gotten slightly tougher, though the inside is still plenty warm and soft. She finds it has a nutty fishy flavor to it with perhaps a slight bite of citrus. It's quite good and swallowing helps sooth the persistent little itch in her throat. She finishes quickly and returns to Danahlia for seconds. The King Centipede is so large the group can eat there fill and still have much of the bug left over. Someone has started to brew some fungus tea as well and once it cools, Lyca, Alice, and Nesu share it.

As they settle down for the night around the fire, Danahlia nudges Alice with her elbow. Grinning, the Liguna nods her head to Twinkaleni, who is drinking from a waterskin, and then casually says, "So, Philip's pretty cute, huh?"

The Murin mage's cheeks suddenly bulge just before water sprays from her nose. They share a laugh at the little mouse's expense, Twinkaleni sputtering and coughing while being roughly patted on the back by Danahlia.

The nine of them fall asleep around the fire as much for comfort as safety, though Alice is awoken by something tickling her nose. She finds Lyca's tail wagging in her sleep, the long fur of it making slight gusts. Alice groans and stills it with a hand. It's very soft and wiggles under her palm for a minute before stopping. Then Lyca rolls over to look at her. She is smiling, Nesu sleeping soundly in her arms still gripping the core stone. Alice grins back and under the soft light of the low fire, drifts off once more.

Chapter 9

Coming Flame

The next morning is full of activity. The camp was in bad shape before they'd arrived but after the battle with the titanic centipede it was in ruins. The huts are a shamble of sticks, everything left in or around them have been scattered and broken. The stones outlining the fire pits need to be regathered, and bits of clay pottery are everywhere.

Lyca rubs the back of her head, seeing the mess in the new day's light and grumbles, "We are gonna be busy today."

At least breakfast is easy. The fire has become a pile of glowing embers, but is quickly revitalized and more centipede on a stick is served. After, Alice goes with Lyca to fetch water, she filling her and her friend's waterskins, while Lyca fills a few relatively intact clay jugs. Looking over at the wolf girl while dunking two skins, Alice can't help but admire her. They are of a similar height, age, and not so dissimilar species, which makes it hard for the young fox not to make comparisons with herself.

Lyca is so strong, leading her group, not following as Alice had gotten into the habit of doing.

And her bravery when she charged the centipede, it inspired Alice, giving her the courage to stand and fight too. She finds herself staring at the Lobovan, wondering what it was that the wolf girl had that she didn't. Lyca catches her watching but Alice doesn't look away, noticing for the first time how green her eyes are. They share a smile before getting back to their tasks.

The pond is nice, large with calm waters, surrounded heavily with trees and topped with a cool mist. The shore slopes a bit, making Alice think it used to be deeper, but it should serve the forest dwellers for a good while yet.

"So, how long you guys plannin' to be in the forest?" Lyca asks casually, focused on her work.

Alice looks to her, lifting an eyebrow, "Tired of us already?"

"No, I'm, just curious. The little magic one said you were just passin' through," says Lyca, finishing her third jug and heading back the way they'd come.

"Twinkaleni, and that was the plan. We can't stay anywhere long."

Lyca purses her lips as if thinking to ask why but then grins, "Well, I hope you can stick around for at least a little bit more."

As she passes behind Alice, she bumps the fox girl's back with her rump, nearly knocking the Tokala into the pond. Alice catches herself, one hand slapping the water, and turns to see the Lobovan saunter away, tail wagging. Alice quickly fills her last skin before chasing after her, eager for revenge.

She catches up to the wolf, and slows, walking beside and just a little behind. She then nonchalantly dumps one of the waterskins over the other girl's neck and down her back. Lyca's mouth and eyes open wide as she stiffens, the cold water soaking her fur. Alice laughs and dashes around her back to camp, waterskins sloshing around her neck and shoulders.

Lyca tries to follow but, with her full jugs, she can only manage a wobbly waddle and calls after her, "Oh, you are so gonna get it, Red!"

When Alice bursts back into camp, she gets the attention of a few of the others, particularly Nesu, who runs up to her asking, "Lyca?"

The small mouse boy had still been sleeping when the pair left on their errand and is clearly distressed by her absence.

"She's comin'," assures Alice, pointing behind her.

Nesu looks to find the Lobovan hobbling after Alice, her legs dripping from where she spilled water all over herself trying to catch up. The young Murin runs to her, complaining about her leaving without him and she tries to console the boy, saying it was only a few minutes. Safe from retribution for now, Alice joins Danahlia and Twinkaleni, handing them their water. The three had agreed to scout a perimeter around the camp to dispose of any lingering floating puffballs and search for more fungi for the healing tea, leaving the forest dwellers free to straighten out their home.

As they set out, Twinkaleni asks how Alice is feeling and if she is suffering from any ill effects after being exposed to the puffball spores. Alice honestly replies that she isn't. The Tokala hadn't thought about it until now, but the subtle dry itch in the back of her throat hadn't bothered her all morning.

"The tea must be working," says Alice, happy to know the others afflicted should be on the mend too.

Twinkaleni nods, "That is good to hear. With that dealt with, perhaps we should consider parting ways with our new friends soon."

"Already?" wonders Danahlia, waving a burning stick around to make after images in the air.

"Yes of course, the sooner the better. Let's not forget we are being pursued. Every day we spend in their company we put them in danger," the Murin mage reminds.

Alice raises an eyebrow, "You mean from that guy from the Order? Why would he do anything to hurt them?"

"I don't know, but why risk it? Perhaps they try to rob this individual as they did us and he takes offense," Twinkaleni explains.

Danahlia waves a negligent hand, "Psh, that guy's probably still in the pixie's forest. I bet Shae and Tally are givin' 'im all kinds o' trouble," then she smirks, "Besides, do you really wanna leave Philip?"

"W-What? Why would he have any part in this decision?" Twinkaleni demands.

"Uh-huh, I saw the way you were checkin' him out on the way here. And hey, I don't blame ya," Danahlia grins, staring skyward as if reminiscing.

Twinkaleni's mouth bounces between a smile and a grimace but then looks away, folding her arms over her tiny chest to grumble, "Absurd," then more calmly states, "He does possess some, admirable qualities."

"Yeah, like being tall, dark, and handsome, I sure noticed," Alice admits, sharing a laugh with Danahlia.

"He *is* rather attractive," Twinkaleni mumbles, unable to help grinning.

"Ha! I knew it!" Danahlia exclaims gleefully.

Twinkaleni sighs, looking down at her feet.

After a few more popped and burned fungi, the girls discuss leaving the forest dwellers and heading on through the rest of the forest. They were fairly well stocked and knew a bit more about this particular wood, which gives them the confidence to believe they would run into little they couldn't handle. Alice doesn't particularly want to leave so soon after making new friends, but also doesn't want to part with the duo that she's shared so much with already. They eventually agree to wait until the sick, at least, were settled in before continuing on.

While making a wide ring around the forest dweller camp, Alice picks up on a familiar scent. Following her nose, she leads her friends to another of the amphora plants and its delightful nectar. Eager for them to taste it, she prepares to pierce the melon like portion with her sword and drain it into a waterskin as Lyca and Nesu had.

"We can drink this?" Danahlia asks, looking into the green, oblong bulb of the plant.

"It smells, lovely," says Twinkaleni, tiny, pink nose sniffing ever closer to the opening in the top.

"Yeah, just don't touch it," warns Alice, lining up the tip of her sword to punch a hole low on the plant.

Danahlia hooks a finger on the lip of the opening to get a better look inside and asks, "Why?"

Immediately, a thick leaf atop the plant falls over the bulb's opening. Curled hairs on the edges of the leaf interlock with the matching set on the bulb's lip, trapping Danahlia's finger.

It being a mere plant, Danahlia easily pulls her finger free and asks, "What's it doin'?"

Alice hadn't seen this reaction before and watches for any more movement.

"Mm, perhaps this is why you were not meant to touch it," chides Twinkaleni.

"How was I supposed to... ugh, uh! What is that?!" Danahlia exclaims as the sweet, fruity, alluring, scent of nectar turns into the horrid, strangely warm, smell of something left rotting in the sun.

Curious about the juice, Alice lifts up the fuzzy leaf covering the bulb to see the inside of it looks to be sweating a milky white liquid that has begun dripping into the nectar. Now opened, the smell quadruples and they all recoil from it, taking several steps back.

"Ugh, I told you not to touch it," Alice complains as they quickly move on.

Twinkaleni rebukes the Liguna too, even as Danahlia argues the innocence of her ignorance.

The trio spends much of the day eradicating more puffballs and foraging. They even manage to collect a bit more of the immature fungi for the healing tea. Arriving back at the camp late in the evening, they find many of the sick children have made the trip, the fungus tea having helped rejuvenate many already. Not long after, Philip arrives with the last of those who needed help making the journey and they're all welcomed with water, food, and cheers. As he walks into camp, they notice he is carrying one of the smaller ones, a Leeseran, on his back. Once Philip places the young squirrel boy down, Lyca gives him a big hug and a kiss on the cheek.

The girls look on, Alice feeling just a hint of jealousy at the display when she hears Twinkaleni sigh at her side, "I suppose we should wait until morning, start fresh with the day."

"Should we tell 'em we're leavin'?" Alice wonders, looking around to see how happy the forest dwellers are to be back and have their friends on the mend.

"Let's hold off 'til tomorrow. No sense in spoilin' the homecomin' party," says Danahlia, a stick of centipede in each hand.

The uncommon abundance of food lets everyone eat without restraint. The fires are kept high while stories of adventures, including the heroic and highly embellished tale of the evil king centipede's fall, are enjoyed well into the night. And for the first time in a long while, Alice sleeps very soundly.

The next morning after breakfast, Alice, Danahlia, and Twinkaleni pack their things, preparing to depart. Lyca appears from the cave with a bow in each hand and a quiver of arrows on her back just as they're putting on their backpacks. She cocks her head to one side and asks, "Where're you guys goin'?"

"Figure your gang's in a good spot now, 'bout time we headed off," answers Danahlia, not meeting the Lobovan's questioning gaze.

"What? But I thought you were gonna stick around, at least for a little bit," she says mostly to Alice, her arms falling to her sides.

"Sorry, Lyca. It's better if we don't stay anywhere too long," says Alice.

Some of the other forest dwellers have over heard and stop what they're doing to listen.

"What's goin' on?" asks Philip, coming to stand beside Lyca and Nesu.

"They're leavin'," replies Lyca glumly, her ears drooping.

Hearing this, Nesu walks up to Twinkaleni and offers her the enchanted core stone he had been holding. Twinkaleni smiles, pushing it back towards him, and telling him to keep it safe for her. The slightly smaller Murin nods and gives her a hug.

"Well, if that's the case, I think we need to send our saviors off as they deserve," announces Philip to a general agreement.

The girls are then given all the food they can carry from Deliduss fruit and Saccha berries to various edible plants and mushrooms, until they simply can't carry anymore. Thanks, goodbyes, well-wishes, and hugs are exchanged, Twinkaleni lingering a bit when she gets her hug from Philip.

Lyca and Alice embrace for a moment, rubbing each others backs, and Alice is surprised to hear the slightest quaver in her voice when she says, "Take care o' yourself, Red."

"You too," she says back. They let each other go and Alice grins, raising an eyebrow, "Is that a tear?"

Lyca sniffs, lifting a finger to her eye, "No! It's just, something... shut up." The wolf girl turns away but then turns right back around, offering out the bow she had been holding, "You can have this. Might come in handy. We can make more so... you know."

Alice's grin widens as she takes it, and then gives the Lobovan another hug, rubbing her face into Lyca's, saying, "Thanks." Lyca's fur is soft, warm, and very pleasant.

"Hey, take it easy," Lyca complains lightly, embracing her back.

After a few more farewells the trio is on its own once more, traveling through the forest. Alice sighs, looking down at the bow in her hands. It's the one she had found in the cave, well made and strung tight.

Danahlia pats her on the shoulder, "I might miss some of 'em just a little bit too," she half smiles looking over to Twinkaleni, who walks grinning dreamily, "I know Twinkie will."

Alice smiles, glad to have had a chance to meet others like themselves, even if only for a little while.

The girls look at the map in an attempt to get their bearings. The forest dwellers had pointed out the direction that would get them to the other side of the forest quickest, but mentioned it would be a walk of several days none the less. Twinkaleni feels this is a good thing, getting more dense forest between them and their pursuer. She prattles on happily about how even if the agent sent by the Order of Thermathrogi had some sort of transport, such as a steed or wagon, a wild enough wood would force them to a slow pace. Alice had assumed the mage hunter would be walking as they were, figuring each step they take is one their pursuer would have to as well. It never occurred to her that they might actually be moving faster.

As they travel, the trio makes a point of popping any floating puffballs they come across. Being very well stocked on food now, there's no need to hunt and Alice figures the load sounds will help keep dangerous ferals away. The forest air is cool and moist, a thin fog ever lingering in all directions. Eventually, the group comes to the stream Philip had mentioned they would encounter. Danahlia checks the shore with her spear and finds that it's as shallow and slow as the Echanian had told them it would be.

Bogged down with all their provisions, their walk has been slow and it's already late in the afternoon. Tired, the girls decide to set up camp beside the stream and cross in the morning. Setting down their things, they make a fire using the burning stick they'd brought from the forest dweller camp and a few dryish twigs and leaves. Eating from their stores, they turn in early so they can start well rested tomorrow.

The next day, when the trio is having breakfast, something bursts from the trees, screeching, "YOU!"

A bipedal monster of some kind launches itself at Twinkaleni while she's filling a waterskin, tackling her into the stream with a splash. The little mouse squeaks and burbles in a panic as the creature attempts to drown her.

Danahlia cries out, "Twinkie!" racing to shoulder charge the thing off of the Murin.

The monster tumbles into the stream and Alice unsheathes her sword, rushing in to deliver a two handed overhead chop, only to stop herself. It's Lyca. As the wolf girl comes to a stop, she lies in the shallow stream making a strange sound, as if gasping for air, moaning in pain, and crying at the same time. Much of her fur on one side of her body is gone, exposing angry red skin patched with ruined brown and black flesh. The fur outlining her exposed skin looks to have been singed.

"Lyca?" Alice whispers, her sword dropping behind her, "What happened to you?"

The question enrages the girl and she tries to rise, snarling at Twinkaleni, "YOU! YOU BROUGHT HIM HERE! HE WAS LOOKIN' FOR YOU!"

Danahlia, unarmed, places herself between the Murin and Lobovan, her hands out and stance wide, "Whoa, calm down! Who?!"

Lyca collapses to her knees sobbing, "He was lookin' for you! It's your fault! It's your fault!"

Alice kneels in front of her, catching the battered girl in her arms and holding her as much to keep her from Twinkaleni as to console, "Lyca! What happened? Who did this?"

"He did. He got everybody! It's your fault!" she wails, flailing weakly toward the Murin mage.

Alice looks back to share a shocked look with the others.

"Who?!" Danahlia demands again.

"Everybody's dead! Everybody's... dead. It's your fault. Your fault," Lyca repeats her anger melting into grief as she slumps against Alice to cry.

"Philip? And Nesu?" Alice asks, shaking the Lobovan by the shoulders. Lyca just shakes her head, tears streaming from wide eyes that stare at nothing, her mind lost in some horrible memory.

"It must be the Order," Twinkaleni sputters, catching her breath, "It's found me at last."

"We, we gotta get outta here, come on," announces Danahlia, splashing to shore to gather their things.

"No, Danny. I can't run anymore. I can't let this happen to anyone else," says Twinkaleni, pointing to the badly burned wolf girl, "I will make my stand here. You and Alice should leave. Take Lyca somewhere safe, he only wants me."

"Are you nuts?! Look what he did?!" Danahlia shouts back, gesturing to Lyca, "We're leavin' and that's that!"

"Fire. Burned everybody," Lyca whimpers in Alice's arms.

Alice pets her, trying to avoid the burned flesh and ignoring the harsh smell. "I'm not going anywhere," she asserts.

Danahlia stamps her foot, swinging her arms in frustration, "Some guy is murderin' kids, with fire! What are we supposed to do against that?!"

"I doubt I can defeat him, but regardless, this ends here," Twinkaleni states stubbornly, moving to check on Lyca.

Danahlia growls, taking her backpack and spear in one hand before splashing loudly toward Twinkaleni. The Liguna picks the small girl up around the waist and begins crossing the stream. The Murin squirms, demanding to be let go, but Danahlia keeps her grip. About half way across, Twinkaleni bites Danahlia's arm and is dropped into the water with an angry shout. The stream is past waist deep on Danahlia, which is too deep for Twinkaleni and she has to start swimming back to shore.

As this is happening, Lyca suddenly starts muttering, "I left 'em. I left 'em," over and over, her nails gouging bloody lines along the sides of her face.

Alice tries to pull the Lobovan's hands away, shouting, "Lyca, stop! There was nothing you could do!"

But the wolf girl is so strong and her mind is too shattered to care.

Alice pries a few fingers away, crying, "Lyca! Stop! Please!"

Twinkaleni is by her side, shaking her head in grim disbelief before saying, "Let us get her to the opposite shore. I will hold the agent off for as long as I am able, you three should flee while you can."

Gathering their things, they try to cross the stream, Alice dragging an unresponsive Lyca until

Twinkaleni can't reach the bottom anymore. She can't swim well with her heavy backpack, so Alice has to pull them both until Danahlia comes to help. Once they're across, Lyca is laid on the shore, the water having washed some of the blood away to reveal the damage she had done to herself.

Dropping her things, Twinkaleni shake dries off and begins asking the wolf girl, "What can you tell me about the man who did this?"

"Come on, guys, let's go," Danahlia pleas, picking up Twinkaleni's backpack.

The Murin shakes her head, "I already told you, I'm staying here."

"I'm not leavin' Lyca like this," asserts Alice, holding the girl's head in her lap and giving her some water, though it just dribbles over her lips.

Danahlia shouts, "Fine! Stay here and get burned alive! I'm outta here!" She stomps away a few yards only to shout her frustration and stomp back, "Come on! We gotta go now! That tick who did this could be here any minute!"

Twinkaleni ignores her and continues trying to get answers from Lyca. She only mumbles something about a red cloak, a golden eye in a triangle, and a glowing ring, before succumbing to fatigue and injury, passing out. The Murin mage sits, rubbing an ear between two fingers as she thinks.

"What're we gonna do?" Alice asks, looking nervously across the stream, expecting to see some terrible figure materialize from the trees.

"Alice, you and me carry Lyca, let's go," Danahlia orders, crouching to put one of the wolf girl's limp arms over her shoulder.

Twinkaleni nods, "I agree. You two need to go."

"You're comin' too, short stuff. Come on, on your feet," the Liguna commands, again reaching out for the Murin.

Twinkaleni pulls away, "No. I will hold him here for a time. If you two are gone before he arrives, he will have no means or reason to pursue you."

"I'm not leavin' you alone," Alice asserts, taking Lyca's other arm.

"You have no choice. I thank you both for coming so far with me, but this is where we must part," says the tiny mouse girl, standing to look defiantly across the shallow stream.

"Ticks! Come on, Alice, we gotta get Lyca outta here," growls Danahlia, pulling the unconscious girl.

"We can't leave Twinkaleni," protests Alice, hesitantly following suit.

"We aren't but we gotta get Lyca outta sight," she says, leading them to a thick tree to place the Lobovan behind before snarling back at the Murin, "You better have a plan for us, pint size."

She does.

Chapter 10

Fire, Water, Wind, and Earth

Twinkaleni's plan has Alice and Danahlia waiting low in the shallow stream. They each have a mass of branches over their heads and try to look like broken tree limbs caught adrift in the slow waters. The mage has selected a spot where the shore line bows out into the water some, predicting the agent will approach there as it is the shortest way across the stream. While Alice and Danahlia wait on opposite sides of the bow, she stands waiting on the opposite shore to lure him in the hopes they will have him surrounded.

Alice pokes her head just out of the water from under her branches, watching the shore nervously while trying not to move. On all fours with the water up to her neck, her fur and clothes are completely soaked and she shivers with fear and cold. Seeing Danahlia's mass of branches further downstream and Twinkaleni standing along the shore comforts her some as she grits her teeth, trying to stop the shaking. They've been waiting for over an hour like this and she's wondering if he will even come, when a figure in a long bright red robe like cloak emerges from the forest, alone and on foot. She freezes, her breath catching in her throat, watching as the figure spots the Murin and stops.

The hood of the cloak is up, hiding the figure's identity, but it could only be the agent sent by the Order of Thermathrogi. All Alice can tell from her vantage point is that the individual is tall, thin, and long limbed. The red cloak shifts as the mage hunter pulls something from it. A hand extends towards Twinkaleni and a roundish bauble drops a few inches from it on a slender chain. The agent speaks a few indiscernible words and the thing at the end of the chain glows a faint orange, moving as if carried by a light breeze in the general direction of the waiting Murin. He replaces the bauble within his cloak and takes a few steps to the shore where Twinkaleni had predicted he would.

"So, I have found you at last. You've led me on a merry chase, mageling, but the end has come. I do give you this choice, little one, return with me of your own will or return with me under mine," the cloaked figure offers in a bored tone.

"I will not return to the Order and neither shall you, murderer!" Twinkaleni shouts from where she stands across the stream.

The man huffs a laugh, "I don't know what you think I am but I am no murderer. Come child, I will take you home. Your masters await." He extends a welcoming hand to the little Murin.

"I *have* no masters! I am free! And *you* killed my friends!" Twinkaleni shoots back.

The man's offered hand closes slowly into a fist before dropping back to his side. "Hmph, friends?" he calls mockingly, "I've merely punished a draft dodger and those who aided him. Any loyal servant of Arsalia would have done the same in my stead. My patience is ended, come to me now."

"They were innocent CHILDREN!" Twinkaleni shrieks, her voice carrying a crack like thunder.

It's enough to rip Alice's attention away from the cloaked man to see her small companion's eyes flare a bright gold, her tiny hands balled into fists. The water along the shore ripples away from her, steadily reaching out to Alice among her branches. The man is quiet for a moment, perhaps taken aback by the sudden surge of raw power, or simply content to let it pass.

He seems to glare at her from under his hood, "Very well. If you will not come willingly, then by the authority given me by Grand Master Igneous Balk of the Order of Thermathrogi, I, Pimine Caine, sentence you, Twinkaleni Orbear, to death. Adarath!"

On the last harshly spat word, the man whips his hand toward the young mage, a gold ring on one finger glowing bright red just as a boulder sized fireball coalesces from within it to fly towards her.

Alice has to force herself to keep from leaping up and calling warning to the small mouse girl. She grits her teeth even harder, hand squeezing the grip of her sword, keeping in mind that it was all part of the plan.

Twinkaleni shouts, "Pavata!" raising both her arms over her head. A wide, squat pillar of water rises from the stream before the massive ball of flame. The two collide with a deafening, searing hiss and an explosion of steam. Warm, almost hot, wet air floods over Alice, mixing with the already present fog, to create a thick haze of water vapor that cuts visibility to only a few feet. This was it.

A split second before Alice throws off her branches, she hears Danahlia shouting wildly from somewhere in the haze. Alice joins in, screaming at the top of her lungs, slapping and splashing the water.

As they try to distract the cloaked figure, Twinkaleni cries, "Feasta!"

Alice sees a blurred beam of orange light race from where she last saw the Murin mage to where the Order's agent had been standing. The orange light hits something, stopping in midair and the man gasps in surprise. Alice goes silent, trying to see through the thick mist, wondering if the attack was successful.

But as the steam slowly dissipates, the man laughs, "Not bad. The Order was right to prepare me for fire."

"The cloak," Twinkaleni rasps and Alice sees the small silhouette of the mouse girl on her knees, the spells exhausting her.

Danahlia charges the man with her spear, splashing toward him and snarling a challenge.

Twinkaleni cries, "No, Danny! Pavata!"

Another thinner but taller pillar rises from the water, this time rushing toward the man as he extends his ringed hand to the Liguna. It's too far, the cloaked man, a red blur to Alice, watches it coming and steps easily out of the way as the water crashes into the ground beside him. Alice, seeing what is about to happen, raises her sword and begins splashing toward the man screaming. But her fur and clothes, heavy with water, make her far too slow.

The man extends his hand again and roars, "Adarath!"

Alice can see the great ball of hellish fire through the haze, fly from the man's hand to burst into the stream with another eruption of steam. Danahlia screams.

"NO!" Alice cries, forcing her heavy legs to carry her onto shore to the man's back. She comes down hard with a chop, but the man turns to catch her blade on a long, serpentine dagger.

He snarls, "Mere children," and pushes Alice's sword away with ease.

Furious, Alice swings her sword as hard as she can, again and again at the tall man, letting anger fuel her strikes. But every time, the man either uses the flat of the dagger to redirect her blows or evades them completely. She slashes and chops at all angles, trying to pierce the man's guard, but the difference in their fighting ability is all too apparent.

Her arms steadily begin to tire, the sword becoming heavier with each swing. The young Tokala's rage turns to fear as the man, smirking, shows how vastly out classed she is. Still Alice swings, now more out of desperation and the terror of what will happen if she stops. Her latest attack is dodged, the man sidestepping, allowing her sword to bite into the soft earth.

He sighs, shaking his head in disappointment, "And I thought bringing in the mageling would prove a decent challenge."

Alice snarls, pulling her sword free and spinning in a full circle to bring the blade around to slice the man in two at the waist. But he steps into her, grabbing her by the wrist with one hand and punching her in the cheek with the other.

The young Tokala's face blooms in pain as she twirls to the ground with a high pitched yip. Instinctively holding the throbbing ache, she reaches blindly for her sword, vision blurring with tears and tasting blood. The man looms over her and shakes his head again.

"At least you tried. Not like your friends at the cave. Just hid and denied ever seeing the mageling till the end," he says, tossing his dagger up and expertly catching it before driving the tip towards Alice's chest.

"Vespis Flowmino!" cries Twinkaleni.

The man glances to his right just as a burst of wind sends him flying several feet away. Alice rolls with the sudden powerful gust over her sword and grips the handle. She sees Twinkaleni fall face first onto the ground from her kneeling position across the stream, the mage's outstretched hands splashing limply into the water. There is no rock or tree for the man to hit and he simply lands on the ground with a pained grunt. Knowing she won't have another chance, Alice takes up her weapon and runs on wobbling, powerless legs to finish the mage hunter before he can regain his feet.

She delivers a chop aimed at the man's head with everything she has left. But the gleaming serpentine dagger meets it in midair. Still, the blow cuts shallowly into the man's shoulder and he growls in pain and anger. The man's hood has fallen back and she can see now that he's a Mustaroni. The weasel man's small sharp teeth grit as he slowly pushes Alice back off of him. Her blade steadily slips free from his shoulder and she bears down with all the weight her slim body has to get it back into him. Then he spits in her eye.

Alice loses focus for only a second but it's enough for him to get a leg between them. He push kicks her in the stomach sending her flying back, Jellybane splashing somewhere in the stream. Alice cries out as she hits the ground, curling around her aching stomach, as she tries to wipe clear her vision. She coughs, unable to get her breath back as the man stands up. He puts a hand to his shoulder and examines the blood on his fingers, his eyes widening with malice. The weasel man then extends his ringed hand to Alice as she cowers away from him on her back and into the water.

"Play time is over. Adara-!"

Lyca leaps onto the man, scratching and biting at his face, her legs wrapping around his chest. He screams under the assault as the burnt wolf girl savages him with claw and fang. They fall to the ground, struggling for a moment until with a vicious jerk of her head, the man's cries become a wet burble. The Lobovan rolls off of him to lie on the ground, her chest red with blood. The man twitches, holding his shredded throat in a desperate effort to slow the life leaving him.

Unable to process what just happened, Alice simply sits in the stream, breathing heavily and watching the man still. Lyca groans weakly, snapping Alice back. She begins to crawl toward her friend, legs and arms numb, face and stomach throbbing, vision blurred with tears and saliva. As she gets within a few feet, she wipes at her eyes to see the serpentine dagger pressed to the hilt, high in Lyca's chest.

She hurries to the girl's side, "Lyca? Lyca?!"

The Lobovan's eyes are still open though they are slow to focus on her. "Red? Did I, get 'im?" she asks, fresh blood dripping free from the corner of her mouth.

"Yeah," Alice sniffs, "yeah, you got 'im."

"Good," Lyca groans, "Why does, my chest hurt, so much?"

"It's nothing," Alice says, trying to figure out if she should pull out the dagger or not, "You're gonna be alright."

"Where's Ne-?" when Lyca doesn't finish Alice looks to see her eyes stare blankly, her mouth hanging open.

Alice sniffs, new tears falling to the Lobovan as she leans over her calling, "Lyca? Lyca?!" she shakes the wolf girl by the shoulders, "Lyca?! Come on! You're gonna be alright! Come on!" She looks for her other friends and spots Danahlia pulling herself slowly from the stream, "Danny! Help! Lyca's hurt!"

Danahlia turns to the sound of her voice and crawls toward her. As she nears, Alice wails, "What are we supposed to do? What are we supposed to do?"

Breathing raggedly, Danahlia looks over the wolf girl and spots the dagger. She shakes her head, and closes the girl's eyes before collapsing herself.

"Danny?" Alice looks to the Liguna to see her generally bark colored back is exposed, clothes burned away, her skin a mess of ugly pink, red, brown, and black flesh. Alice screams, her throat hoarse, "TWINKALENI!" She scans the shore, trying to wipe away tears so she can see but they just keep getting in the way. She calls for the mage over and over, not wanting to leave her friends.

After several minutes with no response, she finally gets up and crosses the stream. Cold and wet, she finds Twinkaleni passed out along the shore. Picking up the little mouse, she also find's their packs where they left them before the battle and lugs all back across. Knowing there was nothing she could do for Lyca, she places a wet bit of clothing over Danahlia's burned back and after a long while gets another fire going. She then uses some more wet clothes to wash the blood from Lyca's body.

Eventually she removes the dagger, revealing the horrible slit it left just over Lyca's left breast. The deceptively heavy weapon reminds her of Jellybane and she wades around in the stream until she finds her sword. She dries the weapon and continues cleaning Lyca off while periodically rewetting the damp shirt over Danahlia's back, her mind blank and movements mechanical.

She is alone again, curling around her mother's arm. Alice had found her in bed one morning after finally starving herself to death. The feeling of abandonment too strong for her to face, the young fox stuck by her mother's side until neighbors came later in the day to check on her. They did often then, knowing it was only a matter of time. Alice knew at some level too but her young mind was never able to prepare. She's jolted from the day dream when Danahlia groans.

It's late in the afternoon now and Alice wipes at her eyes, "Danny?"

The Liguna groans again and looks to see Lyca's still form. "Twinkie? Where's Twinkaleni?" she asks, wincing but suddenly alert.

Alice sniffs, pointing to the slumbering Murin, "She's ok, I think."

Danahlia sees her and slumps back down, "That guy?"

"Dead."

"Lyca?"

"Her too."

Danahlia takes in and lets out a long breath, "You?"

"I'm ok," Alice lies, "How about you? How's your back?"

"Hurts. We got anythin' to eat?"

Alice smiles, sniffing and rubbing a bit of snot from her nose, "Yeah."

They eat and drink as the sun steadily drops behind the trees. Danahlia, not wanting to move much, props herself up on her elbows. Alice had been ravenous but for some reason didn't feel it until now. Looking over to Lyca, she gets the strangest guilty feeling, like she should offer her something. Cleaned off and with one of Alice's shirts covering the wound that stole her life, the wolf girl looks like she's just sleeping. Alice knows better of course but still feels like the girl might rise, hungry after the day's madness, too. She begins to cry again, thinking of how just yesterday they had been playing in the forest. Danahlia comes to sit beside her, pulling her close.

Alice sniffs and asks, "How did things go so wrong so fast?"

"I don't know," the Liguna whispers.

By morning, Twinkaleni is awake and after breakfast they bury Lyca by the stream, digging her grave with their bare hands. The three gather a few wild flowers to decorate the small hill and use river stones to spell out her name beside it. They mourn her for a time before going through the cloaked man's things.

Danahlia puts on his ring, extends her hand out, and calls, "Adarath!" sending a fireball flying into the air, shocking them all. "Sorry, heh, didn't think it was still loaded," she says, taking the ring off and placing it into Twinkaleni's waiting palm.

Twinkaleni sighs and then announces, "It still has some charge left to it, but it will run out eventually."

"Anyway you can recharge it?" asks Danahlia, reaching for the ring, "Never know when a fireball might come in handy."

Twinkaleni puts the ring away into a pocket, "I don't believe my enchanting skills are at a sufficient level just yet, but perhaps in time."

Danahlia frowns and begins trying to remove the man's red cloak. It's embroidered with an eye within a triangle, the corners of which have three smaller triangles, all in gold thread. Alice finds a coin purse with quite a few coins, many of them gold. She pockets this, not feeling the least bit guilty.

Twinkaleni helps remove the cloak and nods, "As I thought, this too is enchanted, very complex."

"What's it do?" Danahlia asks, tugging it roughly off the man.

"Less now, considering the state it's in," says Twinkaleni, motioning to various cuts and tears in the cloth, "But when it was whole, I believe it could dispel, or perhaps even absorb fire." She pulls the ring from her pocket and nods, "Yes, I feel the connection. The cloak could absorb fire and channel it into the ring, keeping it charged."

"That's nice," grumbles Alice, thinking of all the harm the monster had done with this magic.

Twinkaleni sighs, "I'm sorry, Alice. But this could aid us in more ways than one."

"Dibs," says Danahlia without enthusiasm, pulling the ragged bloody cloak from Twinkaleni's hands. As she does, the strange bauble from before rolls free from it and they all look to see what it is. Attached to a thin metal chain is a corked glass globe-like vial, full of orange ooze. Within the ooze floats what might be a chunk of old meat.

Twinkaleni picks it up gingerly, revealing it to be, "A piece of my tail. He was using it to track me."

"Only a piece? Does that mean they can make more of these things?" asks Alice, looking at the shriveled, strange looking hunk of flesh, dark brown through the orange goo.

"Unfortunately, yes," Twinkaleni admits.

"Great," groans Danahlia.

"However, I believe it will be some time before anyone realizes this agent is no longer... operating. So we should have a long while before they even consider sending anyone else, if they do so at all."

Searching through the rest of the Mustaroni's things, they find a few provisions and another knife, this one plainer, more for utility. After a lingering goodbye to Lyca, the girls decide to head back to the forest dwellers' camp to look for survivors, leaving the weasel for the ferals.

Before they even set foot in the camp, late that day, Alice regrets the decision to come. The harsh stench of burning things is still heavy in the air.

"Maybe we shouldn't," says Danahlia, giving voice to Alice's thoughts.

Tears already falling from her eyes, Twinkaleni stubbornly presses on, "I brought this. I owe it to them to at least look for survivors. Lyca made it out, perhaps others did as well."

But as they enter the camp, Twinkaleni falls to her knees. Some of the huts are still smoking, though most are only piles of ash. And before the cave mouth is a large crumpled form whose long blackened muzzle could only be Philip's.

It wasn't real until then and Alice begins to hyperventilate, feeling like she might throw up, as Danahlia tries to pick up the Murin, "Come on, there's nothin' for us here."

"NO! I have to see!" Twinkaleni cries, tearing away from the Liguna to run into the cave.

"Twinkie, don't!" Danahlia calls, chasing after her.

Alice is hesitant to follow, instead kneeling beside Philip's remains, whispering "I'm so sorry."

She reaches out to him but is afraid to touch the rough looking black and red mass that was once a strong, handsome, and kind young man. Then Twinkaleni screams. Alice runs into the cave, but stops almost immediately, finding the rest of the forest children.

They're huddled together in the darkness of corners, blackened feet and hands sticking out from the shadows. Alice tries not to look at them, she doesn't want to see what they've become. Twinkaleni screams again and Alice carefully makes her way to the back of the cave where she sees her friends by the green glow of the unblemished core stone. Tucked in a tight ball at the very back of the chamber is the smallest of the charred bodies, the core stone a few inches from tiny outstretched fingers.

Twinkaleni screams her rage and grief, the sounds echoing into a horrible chorus within the stone tomb. Alice collapses beside Danahlia and joins her in trying to console the Murin mage, failing to control her own emotions.

An unknown time later, Twinkaleni quiets and says in an unexpectedly calm voice, "I'm going back to the Order."

Danahlia exclaims, "What? Are you crazy? After everything that happened, you're just gonna turn yourself in?!"

"No, Danahlia," the Murin mage says, her tone one of finality, "I'm going back to destroy it."

As she speaks, she turns to them, eyes flaring bright gold once more. And for the first time, Alice is afraid of her.

Epilogue

The girls spend the next few days in the forest dweller's camp in the hopes that the survivors may return. After counting the bodies, they know that at least a handful must have fled as Lyca had. That hope is all that comforts them as they bury their friends in earth and tears. Danahlia begins to shed her skin, not only around the massive burn on her back but everywhere. It alarms Alice when she sees it at first, but the Liguna assures her that it is a natural healing process. Alice then helps remove the thin, semitransparent layers of skin and when finished, Danahlia looks somewhat shiny and slick for a time, her back much improved.

They all have nightmares, though Twinkaleni's seem especially terrible. They carry on even after she wakes, often with her repeating, "It's my fault, it's my fault," over and over. Danahlia and Alice have taken to watching her carefully as, periodically, she will spontaneously start banging her fists against her head. She is distracted for a time when she begins scratching a message into a relatively flat part of the cave wall with the utility knife found on the Mustaroni agent.

It eventually reads, "On this spot, the Order of Thermathrogi murdered sixteen innocent, defenseless children." Along with this, Twinkaleni prints as legibly as she can, the names of the victims. Lyca, Philip, Nesu, and several others are already in stone, but then she begins to hit herself again.

Alice pulls her arms away, afraid she'll hurt herself, and when asked what was wrong, the Murin wails, "I can't remember, I can't remember all their names!"

Danahlia and Alice help, and the two have to make up a few, but having sixteen names carved in stone calms Twinkaleni considerably. Once her work is done, the Murin sets the core stone in a rocky dimple so that anyone who passes will be able to see the message clearly in the green glow. The trio manages to find the first camp that the forest dwellers had led them to, wanting to see if the survivors had rendezvoused there instead. They find no one. They leave food out just in case, and cut a message into a tree saying the main camp is safe. They head back to the cave and wait for one more night but no one ever shows.

In the morning, after they set out more provisions in the hopes that someone will return, Alice says glumly, "I think we've done all we can for them."

Danahlia agrees, "Yeah, let's go. We still have a long road ahead."

About the Author:

K.J. Bailey (Kenichiro Justin Bailey) has thus far only written the Alice Dippleblack series, but looks forward to creating more fantastical worlds.

www.ingramcontent.com/pod-product-compliance
Lightning Source LLC
Chambersburg PA
CBHW020557180626
46810CB00007B/2542